Shadow Cursed

The Shadow Accords 2

D.K. Holmberg

Shadow Cursed

ASH Publishing
dkholmberg.com

Chapter 1

The palace walls no longer towered over her as they once had, but Carth still felt the pressure from them, something that was more spiritual than actually physical yet left her wanting to escape nonetheless. The creeping ivy along the side felt like her spirit clamoring to get free of the palace, with the incessant training and the brutality she faced each day.

"If you keep staring at that wall, you're bound to find some fault in it, don't you think?"

Carth glanced to Samis, who lounged near the wall, his sword resting across his legs, a sheen of sweat coating his brow. How long had he been sitting there watching her? Probably too long, she decided, long enough to know how she longed to leave the practice yard and how she longed to climb like the ivy and see the inside of the city. It had been five years since she'd been allowed out. Five years she had remained within these walls, not imprisoned so much as protected.

"What's to find fault with?" she asked. She made a conscious effort to tear her hand away from the hilt of her sword and turned to face him. Though the top of her head might only come to his shoulders, she wasn't about to let him see her intimidated. Mostly because she wasn't—not really—but also because she had to struggle for every bit of respect she'd gained while training and she wasn't about to let Samis Gold take any of it from her. "The ivy is beautiful as it grows along the sides of the walls."

Samis stood and wiped the edge of his blade with his shirt. What was the fool doing with his shirt off anyway? If he thought that impressed her, then he was mistaken. Well… mostly mistaken.

"Who cares if the ivy is beautiful? Look at the stone. That's where the strength is. The ivy doesn't keep you from getting past the wall, does it? That's the stone."

"I would suggest that you are both wrong."

Carth jerked her head around to see Invar Tolneson standing behind them. How had he managed to sneak up on her so easily? All this time, she had been thinking she was getting more skilled, but with one simple act, he made it clear just how little she had learned. She would use the shadows to determine where he was, but the shadow magic had been forbidden from her here. Not because the A'ras thought she shouldn't use it but because these walls somehow blocked her from doing so. It was for her own good, Jhon had told her before leaving her here; because of it, she would learn the A'ras way, and from there she could develop other abilities and eventually merge them with her ability with the shadows. But Carth couldn't help but feel that she was missing something because she hadn't used it for so long. She refused to let herself think about whether she could still even reach the shadows when she crossed to the other side of the wall.

"How is that wrong, Master?" Samis asked. He flipped his shirt over his shoulder as he sheathed his sword. She would have rather seen him cover himself than the sword. At least the sword she could deal with.

"Your assumption is wrong. You believe that it must be either the stone or the ivy."

"You think it's both?" Samis asked.

Invar arched a brow at Samis's casual tone. If Samis was going to attempt such a relaxed attitude with any of the masters, it should not be Invar. Carth wasn't even surprised to see him. Invar had been appearing around her more and more often, which she thought strange, but there was nothing she dared say about it, not to one of the masters.

"I think that there could not be strength without the other. The ivy needs the stone for support, and the stone needs the ivy for its beauty. Yes," Invar said, tipping his head to Samis, "beauty. There is strength in beauty."

Samis touched the leaves of the ivy and plucked one from the vine. He brought it to his nose and sniffed it before tossing it back to the ground.

"Yet it is neither the ivy nor the stone which grants the strength that you discuss."

"What, then?" Samis asked.

"You study with the A'ras, yet you must question what gives strength to the wall?" Invar stared at them intently for a moment. Power radiated from him, as if the man exuded it. With Invar, that was possible.

He turned his back to them and left, crossing the lawn at a measured pace, his hands clasped behind his back.

Samis grabbed a strand of ivy and jerked. The muscles in his arm flexed, giving him another chance to show off, but the vines didn't budge. Some of the leaves fell, but there was nothing else he could do to tear them free, short of unsheathing his sword again and hacking at them.

"You don't care for the beauty?" she asked.

Samis sniffed. "Beauty? These are weeds, Carth, regardless of what Invar claims. They don't do anything to hold the wall. What Invar doesn't say is that it's the A'ras magic that does it, not vines or stone."

Carth couldn't feel the magic in the walls, but that didn't mean it wasn't there. Just because she couldn't feel the shadows didn't mean that they weren't there either. She might not be able to use that magic right now, but she knew it existed, and one day, when she was finally free after her time with the A'ras, she'd be free to reach the shadows again.

Samis jerked his shirt from his shoulder and swung it around. He flashed a wide smile and nodded after Invar. "I think he intends to claim you."

Carth shook her head. "I don't think he claims any students these days." It would be a great honor were Invar to choose her for studies, but it had been years since Invar was said to have taken a student. She doubted he had any interest, and even if he did, she doubted he would choose her.

Samis shrugged. "Maybe he hasn't, but I've seen the way

he watches you, like you're a puzzle he can't quite figure out. What better way to work through a puzzle than to bring it closer, so that it has no choice but to spend time with you?"

Carth shot him a hard look, but Samis completely ignored it.

"Now, I thought we were supposed to practice here. That was the entire reason I came out to this part of the yard," he said.

"You suggested here because you don't want the others to see me defeat you."

Samis's grin faded. "You won't defeat me."

"Like I did Woldan yesterday?"

"That was luck, Rel, and you know it."

She unsheathed the knife at her belt and twisted it in her hand. As she did, she reached for the connection to the A'ras magic, that source deep within her. In the five years she'd been confined within the palace yard, she had spent most of that time trying to master the technique required to simply access the magic. That was the hardest part of truly becoming one of the A'ras. Reaching that power, that source of magic that the A'ras had first believed lay within her, required pulling from a connection that flowed through her veins. She could feel it, the same way she felt it when others used their magic.

Once she managed to master *reaching* the magic, then she could learn ways of connecting to that power and using it for other purposes. The knife helped her hone her connection to the magic, to focus it. Someday, she hoped she would no longer need the knife as a focus, even though many of the A'ras never reached that point. The masters, however, had, and were able to focus their magic without need of an object.

She still couldn't reach that power nearly as quickly as she would like. It came, but it was something like pulling molasses through her veins, trying to separate from her blood, and doing so was *painful*. That was another part of the lessons she'd had to learn: finding a way to reach that power in spite of the pain.

None of the others studying here experienced the same pain. Carth remembered how much it had hurt when she'd first reached the power flowing through her, like her blood had boiled, or had grown too thick for her veins. The masters had frowned when she'd described what she felt, and she remembered all too well how Master Harrison had claimed that any pain was mental rather than physical. Carth found it strange that she still hadn't managed to get past the psychological pain after all these years of studying.

When she'd lived near the docks, using the shadows had required none of the same focus or pain as pulling on A'ras magic. She wanted the same ease that she remembered and even tried to reach for, but the shadows remained blocked to her, possibly by the A'ras magic infused in the walls she and Samis had just been discussing. Her skin tingled, telling her that Samis had reached his magic. He used a short sword—the ashai were not allowed longer or more complex weapons until they were able to craft them on their own— and sent the magic surging into it. Carth's own focus reached her power only a second or two behind him.

But too slowly.

He lunged, swinging his sword, slicing toward her.

Carth ducked, rolling toward the ground, thrusting the long-bladed knife out in front of her, catching his sword and deflecting it to the side. As she did, she *pulsed* through the knife, using that focus to drive power and to push the much larger Samis away.

He went flying, but quickly regained his footing. He gritted his teeth, glaring at her, sweat dripping down his chest. How did he make even battle look appealing?

She forced the thought from her mind. She would *not* allow him to distract her. There were enough distractions as it was. She was too different, her access to the magic too slow, her ability unconventional, but mostly the other ashai thought her too old. She had been when she first came to the A'ras, but now she had progressed to the point that she had nearly reached her age group.

"Nice trick. That's the same thing you did to Woldan yesterday," Samis said. She nodded, pleased in spite of herself that he recognized it. How much attention had Samis been paying to her? "How did you do that?"

She didn't know if he really complimented her or if it was another distraction. "Pushed through the blade."

It was one of the first things she had learned, but she had trouble explaining *how* she did it. Her instructors had never been much help in demonstrating that. They used their blades for focus, but few of them used their magic *through* the blade the way that Carth did. That was part of the reason she struggled to learn some of the techniques that the others so easily mastered—she was hampered by what she could push through her focus, and often it wasn't enough.

Samis held his sword out, and Carth felt the surge of power as he sent it through the blade. He directed it at the ground near her feet, tossing her to the side. When she rolled and jumped back up, he flashed a wolfish grin. "Nice. Now you're in trouble."

He sliced forward, his sword a blur, and sent his magic through the blade, using the technique Carth had demonstrated. If the sword connected, or even if the magic connected, she'd get blasted to the ground, so she had to make certain the sword *didn't* connect with her.

She dropped to her knees and raised the knife up, holding the edge out. As she pulled on her magic, she screamed, tearing it out of herself. There were times when the use of the A'ras magic did not hurt, but this wasn't one of them. It surged in a flash, catching Samis's sword and blocking it, but the force of his blow, combined with the magic he pushed behind it, nearly crumpled her to the ground.

Samis stood over her, more and more power going through his blade. Carth resisted, not wanting to be beaten, and not wanting *him* to beat her.

She pulled on more of her magic. As always, it was like moving molasses when others moved water, and she forced its thick movement through the knife. With a surge of power, she tried pushing Samis off her, but he had been quicker with his magic.

His power exploded, forcing her to the ground.

Carth sprawled forward. Her ears rang and pain coursed through her, leaving her unable to see clearly. Distantly, she heard laughter. She tried to look around to see where it might be coming from, but the pain prevented her from seeing anyone very easily.

Someone grabbed her hand and pulled her up. As her vision cleared, she realized it was Samis. She hated that *he* would be the one to help her.

"That was impressive," he said, his breath smelling of pine and mint. She hated that the scent appealed to her, and reminded her in some ways of her father. "You nearly had me." Samis stepped away from her and slipped his sword into its sheath. "You're strong, Rel, but always a bit slow."

He grabbed his shirt from the ground and flipped it back over his shoulder, turning his back to her as he started away. "Figure out a way to get faster, or you're always going to get beat."

She shot him a hard look that he completely ignored as he continued past her. Carth looked away from the sweat that gleamed off his broad shoulders and tried to ignore the swagger he carried himself with as he made his way back toward the cosak, the low building that housed all the students.

Get faster. That was the one thing she wanted as well, but she couldn't. She *wasn't* fast enough. That was part of the problem with how she reached her magic, the painful way she drew it out from herself. It was different from the others who studied here—*she* was different—and had no evidence she would ever get any faster or better. And if she

9

couldn't, she would never become a full A'ras, and wasn't that the entire point of studying here? Wasn't that the reason her parents had brought her to Nyaesh? She hated how much it still pained her to think of them, hated the knot that formed in her throat as she did, much as she hated that she would never have answers to her questions. Only more questions.

Chapter 2

Carth waited until Samis was completely gone to make her way along the wall, running her fingers along the vines. Shadows flickered. Each time she noted them, she wondered: would she even retain her ability with them if she ever left the palace grounds, or would it have faded from disuse?

Shadow blessed. That was what Jhon had called her, and he'd said he suspected her parents thought her shadow blessed as well. Even though she couldn't ask them, that had to be the reason for the games her father had played with her, the way he'd task her with hiding in the alleys, lurking in the darkness as she made her way through the streets.

His words still called in her head, though with less clarity than they once would have. *Use the dark places to remain hidden. Prevent me from finding you.* When they had come to Nyaesh, she had done that, but she had never managed to keep him from reaching her. Likely, he had been shadow blessed as well. Without the ability to reach the shadows here, she felt more cursed than anything.

As she stood near a part of the wall where it jutted out, she reached for the shadows.

Nothing happened, much like nothing had happened each time she had attempted the same over the last few years. Jhon had suggested she conceal the fact that she was shadow blessed; he'd said that the A'ras would teach her a different magic. But she hadn't realized coming to study here meant she would lose access to her original magic, lose her connection to that part of her that reminded her most of her parents.

Unsheathing her knife, she thought about slicing through the ivy, much as she knew she shouldn't try it. Master Invar had claimed that the ivy had strength, but wasn't it mostly decorative? She'd rather drape it around her shoulders, at least cloak herself in the greenery if she couldn't use the shadows for cloaking.

Standing here, she felt the isolation, the sense of oppression, making her wish she could walk through the streets on the other side even once more, regardless of how dangerous they were. At least here, she didn't have to collect scraps in order to remain safe and to have a place to live. Here she had the protection of the A'ras, a safety she couldn't have imagined when she had lived near the docks, though when she had lived there, she'd feared the A'ras in spite of the freedom she had possessed.

She no longer even knew what things would look like on the other side of the wall. What would she find in the city? There had been challenges, and fear, but there had also been a sense of vibrancy, and life, that living near the palace didn't provide her.

Maybe it would if she were actually given a chance to go into the palace. The ashai were given access to the yard, and they had the cosak, but other than the small building near the wall where classes were held, barely attached to the palace itself, they were not allowed into the palace. Instead, it loomed over them, a reminder of what she could aspire to if she ever managed to match the masters in magical skill.

Her fingers brushed the ivy and touched the cool stone of the wall. From here, she could almost imagine what it was like on the other side. She remembered the danger and the excitement, the dark shadows and their cool caress. In five years, the excitement had probably dulled and the danger increased, but she just knew the shadows were there, waiting for her.

Nyaesh was not her home, but it had felt something like it, if only for a while. With both of her parents dead—killed for reasons she still didn't understand and by a man with abilities kept hidden from her—how could she ever find home again? Studying with the A'ras gave her a place, but that was not the same as finding her home.

Trailing along the wall, she reached the flat part of the grounds. Most within Nyaesh believed the ruling family controlled these grounds and that the A'ras merely provided protection, but she had learned otherwise. The king ruled, but did so with the assistance of the A'ras, and willingly offered the students a place to study and to be safe. A home, were she to want it.

As she stood, staring at the wall, the burning sense of magic raced through her blood.

Carth focused on the draw of energy. The sense of it was familiar to her now, the hot bite of the A'ras magic as it sizzled in the air, drawn from stores within each person, and Carth was somehow able to detect it. Not all were, not even those fully trained. She'd kept her ability from nearly everyone, afraid of what they might say were they to learn that fact. Only her closest friend Alison knew, and that was accidental.

This buildup was particularly potent.

The power was released in a thunder as an explosion tossed her backward, sending her flying until she landed on her back, the breath knocked from her lungs.

Carth scrambled to her feet, and before she knew what she was doing, she started sprinting toward the place where she'd detected the explosion, where she'd sensed magic being used. She probably shouldn't risk this, and she'd probably be chastised for rushing toward a power that was beyond her ability, but with what she'd felt, what other choice did she have?

The explosion had caused a breach in the wall. A narrow gap had formed in the stone, tearing ivy and sending debris scattered across the grounds. A flicker of movement appeared through the breach, and she nearly stumbled. Carth had seen a flicker like that before.

Felyn?

But he was dead, killed by the shadow magic when she'd failed to control it.

Wasn't he?

The flicker appeared again, this time on the other side of the wall.

It happened so fast that she wasn't sure she could believe what she saw.

She slipped the long knife from her sleeve and attempted to use it as a focus. Even though she had trained to pull on her magic, standing opposite a man with powers like the one who had killed her family, she found the focus required nearly impossible to achieve.

The man flickered again. A dark cloak—either a deep brown or faded black—covered him, the hood pulled up over his head so that she saw only his eyes. Another flicker, and this time he stopped.

A pair of knives appeared in his hands, faster than she could blink.

"A trainee? The A'ras send a trainee?"

Carth licked her lips, trying to work moisture into them. She didn't know enough about the A'ras magic to counter a man like this. She knew technique, understood concepts, had mastered both sword and knife beyond what she had ever thought herself possible, but she hadn't practiced enough, not nearly enough.

He flickered again.

This time, she *felt* it as he did. It came like a stirring in her stomach, a nervous fluttering, adding to the nerves already there. Carth dropped and rolled, holding her knife to the side. The blade would be useless against someone with this much power, but what choice did she have but to try?

If she could hold out until others arrived—and she had to believe that others would come, that they would have heard the explosion or detected the breach in the wall as well—then the fully trained A'ras could take over and let Carth slink back to her room to try to understand what had happened.

The man appeared, his knives thrust forward where her belly would have been.

He spun to her, his eyes narrowed. Shadows within his hood prevented her from seeing his face, but she imagined him scowling, imagined him longing to harm her.

With another stirring in her stomach, she rolled again, retching as she did.

The man appeared where she had been, knives stabbed at the ground.

He crouched there a moment and peered around until he found her. "The A'ras do not usually demonstrate such competence. None do, really, which is why they're so easy to kill."

The cold tone to his words sent anger surging through her. Though she had at first assumed the A'ras had been responsible for killing her parents, it had been Felyn, and he had searched the city, hunting for her, hoping to do the same to her. Only because of Jhon's coaching had she managed to escape.

Carth leapt to her feet, holding the knife in front of her. As she did, she sent a coursing of power through it. Either anger or determination renewed her focus, and power surged in the blade. In time, she would learn to make her own, but this knife was the one she'd taken off a powerful A'ras. When she'd come to study with the A'ras, she'd kept it, claiming she'd been given it. No one had questioned her, but then, most of the ashai brought with them weapons they had been given.

The man eyed the knife. He pushed his hood back, revealing closely cropped hair and a long scar running down the side of his face that distorted his spreading sneer.

Carth took a step back. Ivy brushed against her and she could feel the power that still coursed through the wall, even with the damage. As much as she had longed to cross to the other side of the wall, she didn't dare turn around.

"Not only A'ras," he said as he took a step toward her. "I thought we destroyed the others. Could it be that some remain?"

He lunged, flickering as he did when he moved.

Carth reacted on instinct.

Rather than using the A'ras magic, which would be too slow, she reached for the shadows.

It was something she couldn't explain, no different than how she couldn't explain how her body knew to breathe, or how her heart knew to keep pumping blood through her veins. She simply *knew* how to reach for the shadows, even if she had not since coming here.

In the daylight, grabbing at the shadows would have been difficult even when she'd practiced every day. She should not be able to reach them.

But where she stood, ivy created a soft dappling shadow along the wall, and the wall itself created shadows of its own.

Darkness surrounded her as she formed a shadow cloak.

Carth sunk into the depths of the wall, pulling the shadows around her.

She held her breath. Would the man be able to reach her?

"The shadows won't conceal you forever. We have learned ways to disperse them."

He flickered toward her, his knife stabbing at the wall, cutting through the ivy.

Carth started along the wall, trying to move away from him, wanting to put distance between them. Would he see or somehow sense her moving? If he was able to flicker as *he* moved, was it possible he could track her as well?

She should never have run toward the breach in the wall; she should have stayed back and let others come and deal with the attack. What had she been thinking?

The wall pressed forward, one of the decorative pillars bumping against her. Carth took a careful step forward, separating from the wall slightly, trying to hold on to the shadows as she did and maintain the cloaking, but she had been out of practice for too long. The cloak failed.

The man spun toward her. With a flicker, he lunged toward her again.

Carth dropped to the side and rolled.

As she did, power surged, this time a power she recognized: A'ras magic.

Three masters appeared, each with long curved swords unsheathed. Invar was among them, but she recognized Lyanna and Erind as well, both incredibly skilled. They attacked almost as one.

The other man glanced at her almost lazily, then flickered toward the A'ras masters.

His knives moved in a flurry of speed she had witnessed

only one other time, and that had been when Felyn had attacked the A'ras she'd believed to have killed her parents. Before coming here, Carth had thought the A'ras she saw on the streets to be incredibly skilled, but watching the three masters as they attacked, she realized she had never understood the extent of their abilities.

And of the A'ras, Invar attacked with the most skill, using not only his sword, but constant manipulation of the A'ras magic that held the attacker away. The three masters coordinated their attack and managed to surround him.

He flickered.

This time, he appeared near the breach in the wall. He cast one more glance at Carth and winked. "I'll find you again," he said.

He flickered again, disappearing.

Chapter 3

Though light streamed through the open windows within the palace, Carth couldn't get past the darkness that filled her. Not shadows—she would have welcomed the presence of the shadows, and would have willingly called to them—but the combined sense of unease and the feeling of helplessness she'd felt facing the attacker.

Invar and Lyanna led her through the corridors. They hadn't given her the option of returning to the cosak. Right now, she wanted nothing more than to crash into her bed, curl up under the covers, and recover from her exhaustion. After using the shadows again, she didn't know whether it was mental or physical, but what did it really matter? The overwhelming fatigue was real enough either way.

Neither of the masters spoke, and Carth didn't say anything either, not wanting to risk angering them, but she needed answers. She twisted her hands together, debating whether to say anything, before finally speaking. "Who was he?" she asked as they neared one end of the hall.

Lyanna continued onward, but Invar paused and looked

back at her. "I believe he was—is—one of the Hjan."

As he watched her, Carth felt a flutter of nerves through her stomach, much like when she had seen the man flickering, but this time it was only her anxiety. At least, she hoped it was. She'd heard the name before. Jhon had called Felyn one of the Hjan. If she had any doubt about who the attacker had been, or where he had come from, Invar's comment at least helped.

"You've heard the term before," Invar said.

She swallowed, working her dry tongue in her mouth and licking her lips. "I've heard it once."

"It was foolish for you to run to the wall," Lyanna said.

"I was already there. Studying with Samis Gold," she said in a hurry.

Invar frowned. Did he know that she lied, and that she'd run to the spot from which the power had built? "How was it that you managed to subdue him long enough for us to arrive?" Lyanna asked.

Invar had moved a couple paces ahead of them, and he tipped his head, indicating to Carth that he listened.

"I didn't subdue him."

"You didn't die, either. That's more than most are able to claim when faced with one of the Hjan," Invar said.

"I don't understand."

Invar glanced back. "We don't either."

He continued down the hall until they reached an ornately carved door of a deeply lacquered wood. Lyanna paused after opening it—Carth had noticed that she'd used something of her A'ras magic as she opened the door—and waited for Invar and Carth to follow.

The inside of the room looked nothing like what Carth expected.

The hall outside had open windows flooding it with natural light, at least in the daytime. This room had no windows, and an iron bowl in the center of the room held a brightly burning flame. A long table ran through the middle of the room. In addition to Erind, two other A'ras masters sat at the table, as if they had been waiting.

Invar motioned to one of the chairs. "Sit," he said.

Carth swallowed. What had she done to get called in front of the masters? As far as she knew, her ability with the shadows was not known, so maybe she had upset them by using it against the attacker.

She took a seat, perching herself on the edge of the hard wooden chair and clasping her hands on her lap beneath the table. She stared down at her legs, wishing again that she could return to her bed, that she could simply sleep. As soon as this was over, she would.

"Erind claims they have returned to the city." This came from Harrison, one of the oldest of the A'ras. With his gray hair and wrinkled eyes, he looked more grandfatherly than terrifying, but when he worked with the students, he was incredibly hard. She feared him nearly as much as she feared Invar.

"So it seems," Invar said.

He took a deep breath and set his hands on the table. With a surge of power, an image formed between them, and Carth gasped. She'd never seen the A'ras use their magic in quite this way. She could see the details of the man attacking as Invar replayed the attack, where the three masters had surrounded him, forcing him to retreat. When the man flickered and disappeared, Invar pressed his hands together, and the image faded to nothing.

"The last attack was—"

"Five years ago," Invar said, glancing down the table and looking at Carth.

"We were unable to confirm the Hjan presence that time," Malasi said. With her peppered brown hair and rich, almost chocolate eyes, she had much of the coloring of Carth's mother.

"Unable to confirm? What did Avera tell us?"

"She claimed the man was Hjan, but we had no proof. No body, in fact," Harrison said. "And now she has departed the city. Unfortunate that she should be gone when we might have need of her knowledge."

"It was not my decision to send her from the city," Invar said.

"We could not keep her in the city, Invar," Lyanna said softly. It had the sound of a familiar argument. "Besides, she's sent word that she will soon return."

"We knew what risk we faced—"

Harrison cut him off by raising his hand. "Not now. This is not the time for such discussions. If they have attacked in the city—"

"And if they do so again," Erind said, "it means they likely side with the Reshian."

Invar frowned at him. "We don't know that."

"We don't know this was them. The Reshian could have done this."

"You mistake their ability—" Invar started.

"One was here before," Carth said. She pulled her gaze from her lap and forced herself to at least look at Lyanna, but the woman wouldn't meet her eyes. Invar watched her, his deep frown making his face look more angry than anything. "I saw one of the Hjan before. Fought one. His name was Felyn. He killed my parents."

"Felyn?" Harrison said. He glanced at the others until Malasi nodded.

"There were rumors of a Hjan named Felyn, but I had not heard that he came here."

"How did he get through the wall?" Carth asked.

"We all knew the rumors five years ago. Many died," Malasi went on, as if she hadn't heard Carth.

"Rumors only. There is no way one man could have killed as many as were claimed," Harrison said. "Perhaps they were working with the Reshian even then."

Invar spread his hands again and the image of the attack reappeared. "This is what we faced. One less of us, and we might not have been enough."

"How did she manage to hold him off?" Harrison asked, looking at Carth.

They all turned their attention to her, as if finally seeing her. Carth brought her hands up to the top of the table and squeezed them together. "I didn't hold him off."

"You're still alive," Invar said again.

"Luck. When he… *flickered*"—she didn't know a different

word for what he'd done—"it was like I could feel it. I was able to get out of the way before he hurt me."

She doubted she would have managed to do so for much longer. Had the masters not come, she would have been stabbed, or attacked by his strange magic in some other way, maybe left to bleed out onto the grasses of the grounds much like her mother had been left to bleed out onto the cobbles of the street.

"Impressive luck," Invar noted.

She nodded, not wanting to look up. She wouldn't have survived if not for the shadow magic, but she could hardly tell the masters that. Jhon had warned her not to use her magic here, told her that she would need to rely on the magic that she gained with the A'ras instead.

"How did he get through the wall?" she asked again. "You said it was strong, and I can feel the power in it."

"You can feel it?" Malasi asked, leaning forward.

Carth nodded carefully, looking at Invar, then back to Malasi. If any others were able to feel the A'ras magic, it would be the masters. "That's how I knew about the attack. I felt it building and then... then the wall blew in." She turned back to Invar. He seemed the most likely to answer her questions. "How was he able to do that? Who are the Hjan?"

"They are collectors of power," he answered.

"You should not—" Harrison started, but Invar turned to him and shot him a hard look.

"What kind of power?" she asked. Carth knew she shouldn't speak so freely, especially around the masters, but how else would she learn what she had faced? All those years ago, Jhon hadn't answered her, but then, she might not have been ready. She certainly wasn't old enough to know if she was ready for the answer.

"The kind the A'ras possess. Others possess different power. The Hjan would understand it all."

"That's why they came to the palace? Why they attacked the wall?"

"I don't have the answer—"

The door slammed open and another A'ras staggered in. She was a compact woman, and dried blood covered her face. She glanced at the assembled masters in the room before her gaze fell on Carth and her eyes widened.

Carth recognized the woman. She was the A'ras who had helped Jhon when they'd faced Felyn, the one who Carth thought had hunted her through the city. And perhaps she *had,* but not for the reason Carth had suspected at the time. She had wanted to test Carth, offer her the opportunity to study with the A'ras if she passed.

"Avera?" Lyanna asked. "What happened?"

The woman shook her head. "We need to protect the palace. They're coming."

"The palace is protected, Avera. Sit. We'll find a healer and get you help."

"There is no time. I barely managed to escape. The attack—"

"We have already been attacked," Invar said as he stood. He slipped an arm around Avera and guided her to the table, helping her to sit in the chair he had occupied.

She looked around the table. "Already attacked? Did they get it?"

"What are you talking about?"

Avera took a deep breath. Power surged through her as she did, a heat flowing through Carth's veins as she became aware of the magic Avera used. As she did, Avera calmed herself. "The Reshian. They attack. I have only barely managed to get past them."

"Reshian?" He looked over at Carth, his face troubled. "They weren't a part of any attack. It was Hjan, and we stopped the attack. He thought to breach the wall—"

Avera leaned forward. "He? No... there were dozens. You haven't stopped anything yet. And we can't let them reach what they seek."

Chapter 4

Carth sat in her room in the cosak, her legs drawn up to her chest and her eyes staring out the open window as she focused, listening for sounds of another attack. So far, none had come, but Avera had made it clear that something would happen. According to her, they hadn't stopped anything, only delayed it.

The idea of something worse than the Hjan—and from the reaction of the masters, they believed the Reshian *were* worse—terrified her. Other than Invar's claim that he had resealed the wall, what prevented even the Hjan from simply flickering back onto the grounds and attacking again?

Stranger to her was the idea that the Reshian would possess some kind of power. She had known about the Reshian and the A'ras warring, but it had never been anything more than a distant battle, one that she was not a part of. If the attack reached the city, it became something she needed to understand. She should have asked questions long ago when she lived with Vera and Hal. They had brought in Reshian strays, which meant they knew something about the Reshian attack.

A knock sounded on her door, but she ignored it, instead letting her focus drift outside the window, trying to reach for the shadows. At least with that connection, she felt like there might be something she could do to hide. With the A'ras magic, she couldn't do anything—she'd barely *done* anything—but with the shadows, she *could* hide.

But did she want to?

The knock came again, this time with more urgency. What did it matter if she answered? Likely it was only one of her friends, or maybe even Samis come back to taunt her again, but she was in no mood for that, so she ignored it.

She couldn't ignore the attack on the palace. As much as it had frightened her—and it had—Felyn had killed her parents. And if the man who just attacked was to be believed, he had killed others like her. Could she sit back and do nothing if she knew?

The knocking stopped and the door opened.

"You *are* here!"

Carth glanced over to see Alison standing in the doorway. She was two years younger than Carth, but looked twice that. Her blue eyes were so faint as to be almost white, matching her pale skin. Only her hair was dark, nearly jet black and beautiful. Up until a year ago—when Carth had risen far enough within the A'ras to earn her own room—they had been roommates. Now Alison had another roommate, but still came to visit Carth as often as she could.

"I'm here," Carth said, looking back out her window.

"What *happened*?" Alison asked, leaning on the foot of

Carth's bed. She didn't seem to notice the way Carth stared out the window.

"What do you mean?"

"Everyone is talking about how Invar came looking for you!" Alison seemed far more excited about this than Carth, but then Alison had a hard time being anything *but* excited most days.

"Invar came for me, but that was because of the attack."

That calmed Alison. "Attack?"

Carth blinked and turned to her friend. Alison sat on the foot of the bed, running her fingers though her long black hair before tucking it into the back of her shirt. "Isn't that why you came?"

"No. Samis claims Invar wants to teach you. I thought I'd come and find out whether that was true or whether he's just messing with me. Invar hasn't taught anyone for *years*, so why would he offer to teach you? Not that I would blame him for wanting to work with *you*," she said quickly.

Carth waved her hand dismissively. "Invar didn't make any offer to teach me. That's just Samis reading into the fact that Invar approached both of us when we were near the wall."

Alison grinned. "What were you doing at the wall with Samis?"

"Not what your mind would think. I was there and he came by. Thought he'd flash himself around without his shirt on, as if it would impress me."

"It'd impress me," Alison said.

Carth laughed and stood, going to the window. She

leaned out, searching for anything that might indicate the use of A'ras magic. Or any magic, for that matter. It didn't matter if it was A'ras. What she really worried about was whether she could detect the Hjan magic. Or the Reshian, though she didn't know what kind of magic they possessed. "I think Samis would impress you dressed for the Nhalin Fjords."

"I don't know where that is."

Carth closed her eyes, remembering the book of her mother's she'd seen all those years ago with maps to places that were impossible to believe existed, and yet... they *must* exist, much like Ih-lash existed in more places than her mind. That was her homeland, and though she had no memories of it, her parents had often spoken of it in ways that made her feel like she knew what it had been like.

"North. Far to the north, and across the Saolin Sea."

Alison laughed nervously. "Are you making that up?"

Carth took a deep breath, thinking of the maps, and the hint of the snow she remembered, like nothing more than a dream, as they had traveled for Nyaesh. She had never understood why her parents had chosen this place—why they had been so determined to reach it—until long after they were gone. She now believed they'd come here so she could study under the A'ras, but what if that wasn't really true? What if it went against everything they would have wanted for her?

"And what if I am?" she said, forcing a hint of humor into her voice. Alison didn't need her moping, and there was nothing her friend could do other than try to cheer her up.

"You've barely ever been outside of Nyaesh, so you wouldn't even know what the fjords were like."

Alison grinned. "I've read, too. I still think you're making it up, and I still say that I wouldn't mind seeing Samis wearing anything." Her grin faded as Carth didn't react to her comment. "There really *was* an attack."

Carth nodded. "There was."

"Where? When? Wouldn't we have heard of it?"

Alison's concern about the attack would be amusing under other circumstances. The A'ras were tasked with providing a level of protection through the city, and they did so with force, using their magic to provide protection and stability. At least, they had. Now that she had seen the risk that the Hjan posed to the A'ras—twice—she wasn't sure how much protection the A'ras could really provide.

"The yard. It was after Samis left. I... felt... a buildup of power." Alison was one of the few who knew of her ability to detect power shifting. Alison arched a brow at her but didn't say anything. She knew that even with the ability, Carth had only a general ability to detect *where* the power came from, which was why she had run toward the wall.

"You felt power. And then there was an attack?"

Carth nodded. "I was the first one there. The man who attacked... he managed to get through a breach in the wall."

"That shouldn't be possible!"

"I know that."

"No. You didn't grow up in the city, so you might not know the history. The walls were placed by the earliest of the A'ras. The masters fortify them every month. They're designed to keep us safe. That, and to keep others safe from us when we're practicing."

Carth hadn't considered that would be a benefit of the wall, but now that Alison mentioned it, it made sense. The wall *would* protect those within the city from the students struggling to learn their magic.

"And you say that only one person penetrated the wall?"

"There was only one there. Avera thinks others are coming." Not Hjan, but something she feared as much.

"Which is why you've been sitting here staring out your window. Do you really think there's anything you could do if there was an attack?"

She didn't, which was the reason she sat and stared out her window. The fact that there had been nothing she could do against the Hjan attacker... that had left her scared. She had managed to hide, but she hadn't been able to do anything more. She'd have thought that, after all the years she'd spent here, she would have learned enough to protect herself, but she was just as helpless as she had been when her parents were taken from her. In the months after they were gone, she had learned to use the shadows, but even that wasn't an option here, not while learning A'ras magic behind the wall.

"Come on," Alison urged. "You promised me you would work with me this week and not spend all your time with Samis."

Carth shot her a frown. "I didn't *want* to be with Samis. We've been paired to practice together."

Alison grabbed her arm and pulled her up. "Don't act

like you weren't interested in practicing with him. I'm pretty sure there are plenty of others who would want to work with Samis as well." She grabbed Carth's maroon sash, which marked her as an ashai, and waited while Carth tied it on. As she progressed—if she progressed—she would be granted different lengths of sash, until she reached a point where she could choose whether she even wore one. Some masters, like Invar, she had noticed, didn't bother wearing theirs. Invar didn't do much that he didn't want to do.

"I'm only doing what I was asked to do."

Alison laughed as she reached the door. "That sounds nothing like the Carth I know."

She hesitated until Carth followed.

Had Alison not come, Carth would have preferred to sit and stare out the window of her room, but that wouldn't solve anything, nor did it do anything to make her feel any better. In some ways, she felt worse. Not telling Alison about her ability with the shadows bothered her. Ever since Carth had come to the A'ras to study, Alison had been her friend. She was one of the first people Carth had met, and they had made an immediate connection. Not because of shared experiences at the time—Alison was born in Nyaesh, where the A'ras magic was more common, and had always hoped to join the A'ras. Her parents had openly pushed her toward it, whereas Carth's parents had intended to sneak her into the A'ras but never revealed their plans. Had she known, would she have tried to make it to the A'ras after losing her parents, or would she have done the same as she had and found a place to hide?

Alison guided her out of the cosak until they reached the yard outside. Carth felt the presence of magic pressing all around her, but none of it had the same focus as it did when the masters used it. With the students, and especially with the younger students, the power they used was less coordinated in some ways. There was power—some of the students had enormous potential with their magic—but often none of the same control, nothing like what she'd seen when Invar and the other masters had fought off the Hjan.

"Where are you taking me?" Carth asked.

"I want to see the wall," she said.

Carth stopped and Alison turned back to face her. "I don't think that's a good idea."

"They repaired it, right?"

Carth nodded. "They repaired it. At least, that's what they told me. But I don't think we should go back there."

She didn't like the idea of returning to the place she'd been attacked. All it would accomplish would be to remind her of her inability to do anything to stop the man who'd killed her parents, and she didn't need that reminder. The nightmares she had too many nights were enough for that. At least she'd managed to conceal *those* from Alison.

"Come *on*," Alison urged. "If there's a whole collection of masters there, we'll turn back."

A part of her *wanted* to return to the wall, if only so she could see if she could reach the shadows again. The breach had disrupted the A'ras magic that prevented her from reaching the shadows. Would she be able to reach past the magic and access that power again?

"Fine, but I'm not going to explain to the masters why we came if we're caught, so you'll have to come up with a good reason."

Alison paled slightly and then laughed. "There won't be any masters there. How often do they ever make it outside the palace?"

Not often, Carth knew, which made Invar coming into the yard that much more uncommon. She could understand why rumors would spread about him seeking to teach, especially thinking that he had left the palace almost as if to seek her—or Samis, she had to admit—out.

"Besides, you're almost sai. When you reach that level, you'll get to leave the grounds and start your first assignments."

"I've got a ways to go before I reach that point," Carth said. The sai were the first level of A'ras, and they were allowed on assignments, no longer restricted to the palace grounds. Most sai were at least eighteen, but then, most of the sai had been studying with the A'ras since they were eight. Carth hadn't come until she was twelve.

Alison frowned. "I think you're closer than you admit. Even the sai A'ras continue their lessons, only they no longer have to remain in the cosak for training. You're almost there. You'll be closer if Invar claims you. Once you get a master to work with, you're basically one of the sai."

"I'm not like you," she said. "You've been here how many years? Seven? I've been here five. There's still so much to learn."

Alison shook her head. "You should see the way others

watch you, Carth. We all know you have the potential to become one of the masters. All it takes is time—and if Invar chooses you, it won't take much of that."

"It's not potential, it's speed," she muttered.

Alison laughed. "So what if it takes you longer to reach your power if you can access more than others when you do?"

"It matters," Carth said. "If I'm killed before I can reach it, it matters."

They reached the flat area leading up to the wall where she'd been attacked. As Invar had said, the hole in the wall had been repaired, the stone replaced, and power surged through the walls once more, rubbing against her like a vibration within her blood. It lacked something, though Carth couldn't quite put a finger on what.

"This was where the attack occurred?" Alison asked.

Carth reached the wall and realized what had felt out of place. Ivy was shredded, with strips of vines and fallen leaves where the wall had been damaged. She ran her fingers along the ivy, wondering if it really had much of an impact on the magic contained within the wall.

This late in the day, the sun cast strange shadows, leaving the ivy with a dappled appearance with dark patches that appeared and then disappeared. Carth felt drawn to these shadows, drawn to run her hand along the vine. Could the vines really augment the magic here?

"Look at this," Alison said. "When you said the attack had destroyed a section of the wall, I didn't think you meant a section this large!"

Carth nodded, still focused on the shadows along the wall. They were more prominent than what she remembered seeing before, and she felt compelled to reach for them, to see if her shadow magic would work.

"How do you think they managed to destroy this section of the wall?" Alison asked.

Carth pulled on the shadows before she realized what she was doing. They surged around her, swirling into the shape of the shadow cloak she'd long ago discovered how to form.

Alison looked past her. "Carth?"

Had she concealed herself with shadows? She shouldn't be able to do that here, not with the A'ras magic holding back that aspect of her abilities. Had the attack somehow freed something for her?

Alison turned away and Carth released the shadows. "I'm here."

Her friend frowned. "Where did you go? You were here and then... then you weren't."

"I was just near the wall. You probably overlooked me."

Alison frowned, her face making it clear that she couldn't tell whether Carth played a trick on her, and started to say something when energy burned within Carth, pressure building from the use of magic.

"What is it?" Alison asked.

Carth shook her head. "I don't know."

"I've seen you make that face before. You felt something, didn't you?"

She nodded carefully, feeling the release of the power. As she did, she couldn't shake what Avera had said, and how she thought others would attack again. Had they reached the palace already?

"If you want to go check it out…"

Carth looked toward the palace, then shook her head. That would only expose her to more questions, and after the way the masters had treated her, she wasn't sure she wanted that.

As they started back toward the cosak, Carth felt the subtle pull of the shadows. Stranger still, it seemed something else pulled *against* the shadows as well.

All these years and she hadn't detected it, and now she could. Had the Hjan attack defeated the A'ras ability to suppress the shadow magic, or had the attack changed something for her?

Chapter 5

The next few days passed mostly in a blur. Carth endured the classes with the instructors and mostly managed to stay away from Samis and his friends, but she couldn't shake the rumors. Most had heard about the incursion and heard that Carth had been there. It was bad enough that someone had broken through the palace wall—and the rumors about who and how ranged from impossible to ridiculous—but worse that Carth had been there for it.

At times, she thought maybe she could reach the shadows again. She'd managed it twice that day, the first time when attacked, and the second when Alison had dragged her to the wall. Since then, she might have tried to reach them, but she hadn't managed to do so. As much as she wanted to use the shadow cloaking, she wondered if maybe it was better that she didn't. That way, she could focus on what she was supposed to be doing, and use the power she was supposed to be learning.

Samis approached her on the second day after the attack, finding her near a small copse of trees during a break in the day's lessons. Carth worked on focusing, trying again to reach for her magic, but was distracted by the tickling sensation of something else at the back of her mind. She didn't know what that something else was, only that it was there.

"You saw it, didn't you?" he asked.

Carth, who had been concentrating on her knife, trying to pull the A'ras magic, looked up. As usual, the magic came slowly, but almost more slowly the last few days, as if her entire focus was off, which it was. In order to regain her focus, she needed to study, to sit back and figure out how she could push past the restrictions she seemed to have placed on herself, but she didn't know how.

Samis was dressed in a loose shirt with the top few buttons open. His maroon sash was tied around his arm, almost too tightly. A part of her wished it would cut off the blood flow to his arm. Maybe that way she could beat him in their little battles, but even then she'd probably fail.

"The attack?" she asked.

Samis sat next to her, shifting his sword off to the side as he did. "Like you really need to ask. That's all anyone can talk about. You know the rumors have it that it took five masters to fight the attackers off?"

Even though she knew he fished for information, she didn't care. "It was only one attacker."

His eyes widened. "One? And they took on *five* masters?"

"Not five. Three."

He whistled softly. "Still. Three masters against one. What kind of magic do you think he used?"

Carth shook her head. She'd tried not to think of what magic the Hjan were able to reach, knowing that same magic had allowed Felyn to kill her parents, and had nearly killed her. "I don't know. Something plenty powerful," she said.

Samis whistled again. "Powerful probably doesn't fully explain it, I'd bet." He turned to her, a curious smile tilting his lips, his blue eyes nearly piercing. "How'd you survive it? Rumor has it that you were the first one there. If that's the case, and if this attacker managed to fight off three of the masters—and survive—how'd you live?"

Carth had spent the past two nights wondering the same thing. How was it that she had lived when the masters had barely forced him away? But then, she hadn't really been trying to fight him off. She had been trying to hide from him, using whatever magic she possessed that would keep him from killing her. Thankfully the darkness had helped her then, even if it wouldn't—or hadn't—helped her since.

"I got lucky," she answered. "Besides, I wasn't there that long before the masters arrived. He tried to stab me and I ducked. That's pretty much all I did." That was mostly true, at least. What did it matter that she'd also managed to use the shadows to hide herself from him?

Samis studied her, his gaze intense enough to make her uncomfortable, and then smiled. "That is lucky. What was it like?"

"Terrifying," she answered quickly.

"Not that. Watching the masters fight. What was *that* like?"

Carth hadn't taken the time to appreciate what she'd seen.

"They were... impressive," she said. "Powerful. I haven't seen anything like it before."

Samis whistled again and let out a long breath. "What happened? I mean, what *really* happened, Rel?"

She gathered her thoughts before speaking, pausing long enough to debate whether she would even answer. If she did, she'd be satisfying his curiosity, but it might help her in some ways as well. Samis would share with others. "The man... he attacked with power. When I said that I got lucky, I really meant it. I almost didn't get away. Had it not been for the three masters, I wouldn't have survived." She pulled her knees up to her chest and shivered.

Samis turned to her and fixed her with that intense gaze of his, deep blue eyes meeting hers and making it hard to turn away. "What do you want the others to know?"

She frowned. "I don't care what the others know, Samis. Let them think whatever they want about the attack for all I—"

He rested his hand on her arm, silencing her. "Assage knows I don't know what it was you saw, and with the way you're treating me..." He shrugged and lifted his hand from her arm, leaving a residual warmth behind. "I figured I could keep others from bothering you if you wanted. That's it."

Carth didn't know what to say, shocked that Samis had made an offer that seemed almost *decent*. "Tell them whatever you want," she said. "Doesn't matter anyway. Most probably think I did something to trigger the attack."

Samis chuckled softly. "Some do. I can't promise that whatever I'd say would change their minds. They don't *know* you, Rel. You keep to yourself and never share much." He shrugged again. "Things might go easier for you if you tried to get to know others."

"I try," Carth said.

"You try. You're friends with Alison, and that's about it. She's nearly as…." He seemed to catch himself and grinned.

Carth didn't need him to finish. Most of the ashai—at least those who were close to her level—thought Alison was almost as odd as Carth. Maybe that was why the two of them worked as friends, though Carth liked to think it had more to do with the fact that they treated each other decently—much better than the rest of the ashai treated them.

"Thanks for the offer," Carth said, getting to her feet.

Samis looked up at her, his stupid deep blue eyes practically seeing through her, but she refused to let him get to her. The only reason he'd come over to her now was to try to find out some gossip about what had happened during the attack, and she'd been foolish enough to share—and share more than she should have.

"Hey," he said, and she paused. "Next time we spar, I might be one of the sai."

"You've been tested?" she asked.

A smile spread on his face. "In two days. Don't worry, I'll still come around to show off for you."

He winked, and she stormed off before saying anything more to him, ignoring the glances of some of the others sitting nearby. They'd ask Samis what he said to her later anyway.

Alison found her as she reached the cosak. "What happened?"

"Nothing. Just Samis trying to find out about the attack."

"That's not surprising. I think everybody wants to know more about what happened. You've become famous for it, as if you needed any more fame."

Carth stopped and crossed her arms over her chest. "What's that supposed to mean?"

"Don't glare at me like that, Carthenne Rel!"

Only Alison knew her full name, and hearing it used it like that forced a smile out of Carth. Her mother had never used anything but her full name, but her father had shortened it, referring to her as Carth, and occasionally Thenney. That was a nickname she refused to share with anyone else; it belonged to her father.

"I'm sorry! This whole situation is frustrating. As if it weren't bad enough that Samis beat me so publicly—"

"That wasn't public."

Carth arched a brow at her. "Really? How is it that nearly a dozen people have stopped to ask me when I'd face Samis again?"

"Well, it *is* Samis, and you're… well, you're Carth. They know they'll get a performance."

"I'm not as skilled as Samis," Carth said.

"Not as fast. But I think we can both agree that when the magic works for you, you're his equal."

When. It was so rare that her magic worked quickly enough for her to be anyone's equal, and certainly not Samis Gold's. Carth knew he had studied here for much longer than most, coming to the palace when he was barely five because the A'ras had detected significant talent in him from an early age. That gave him seven years of study on her, seven years during which he'd learned not only to reach his power, but to use it in more creative ways.

"Anyway, you can't let the others bother you."

"How? How is it that you manage to smile through everything they want to put you through?"

Alison shrugged. "I remember that the A'ras chose me. They detected magic within me. I'm meant to be here, Carthenne Rel, the same way that you're meant to be here."

Carth wondered about that. The A'ras who had granted her admission might have detected magic in her, but how much of that was from the shadow magic, and how much of it was from an ability to use the A'ras magic? It was an answer she doubted she would ever get.

"Let's get something to eat and ignore them. Well, you can ignore them. I'd prefer to study Samis Gold a little bit. His hair, or the way he looks at you with his deep blue eyes… maybe you can spar with him again and convince him to take his shirt off?" Alison smiled playfully. "No? Worth a shot, don't you think?"

"You can keep Samis."

"I would," Alison said with a smile.

"At least one good thing came from the attack," Carth said.

"What?"

"Master Invar hasn't come and watched me like he'd been doing. It makes me uncomfortable with the way his eyes go unfocused, as if he's seeing through me."

Alison laughed and shook her head. "You *are* strange, Carth. You know that most ashai would be thrilled to have Master Invar studying them? Getting the attention of *any* of the masters is a big deal. With something like that, you might even be able to skip serving as sai and move straight into serving as elui. That's only a few steps away from training for master rank!"

Carth sniffed. "I don't know that I *want* to train for that. I'd be happy reaching sai so that I can leave the palace grounds."

"Why would you want to leave the grounds? The city isn't all that safe. You of all people should know that."

Carth nodded, keeping her eyes closed as she thought of her parents. "I wonder if it's not better to be free in the city than to be confined here."

"You'll not always be confined. And you'll have to face the streets outside the palace grounds soon enough. We all will. Enjoy the safety while you can."

As they stepped inside the cosak, Carth shivered. Why would the A'ras need to infuse so much power into the walls? What reason would there be other than to prevent something the A'ras feared from entering?

If that was the case, did the A'ras *expect* another attack like the last? Had they expected the first attack?

Alison nudged her, seemingly knowing the troubled thoughts that rolled through Carth's mind. Carth forced a smile, trying to convince her friend that she was fine, but she wasn't sure if she succeeded.

Chapter 6

Another few days passed, and in that time Carth made a point of avoiding everyone she could. She heard the whispers behind her back, though, whispers that told her how much Samis had shared. Enough that others looked at her even more strangely, if that were possible, and enough that she heard the words "three masters" more than once. A few even cast pitying looks in her direction, but she made a point of ignoring them much like she ignored every other look she got.

"Don't mind them," Alison said softly as they hurried from the cosak. Carth had gotten a few more strange glances in the dining hall, which she'd tried hiding from by staring at her food, but she couldn't hide from all of them.

"I don't mind them," Carth said.

Alison offered her a weak smile. "It'll blow over."

"I know." And then they would move on to something else strange that she'd done. The ashai were a small enough group—barely fifty all told—that she couldn't hide from everyone. They were also small enough that the A'ras did all

48

they could to train any with potential.

"What do you want to do? I hear Samis is facing two others today. Now that he's been raised to sai, it might be fun to go watch. Chances are good that he'll lose."

Carth laughed in spite of herself. "If Samis loses something like that, I'd be surprised."

"You managed well enough against him."

Carth shrugged. As she did, she felt a buildup of power that burned through her veins. She'd detected similar buildups several times over the last few days. Ever since the attack, really. Each time, they'd diffused and she felt nothing further. This time was similar... but also different.

Her stomach fluttered, and for a moment she thought she might retch.

"Are you okay?" Alison asked.

Carth turned to the side, covering her mouth. The last time she'd felt like this was when she'd detected the Hjan attacker.

She looked up. If the Hjan had returned, did the masters know?

Of course they would know. They would have to, wouldn't they?

"Do you feel that?" she asked Alison as the nausea eased. It left her for a moment, and then returned worse than before. She couldn't help herself and retched.

Alison stepped away. "I don't feel anything, but it looks like you do. Let's get you back to your room—"

Carth wiped her arm across her mouth. "No. This is like the last time. This is what I felt."

There came another surge of power, this time one that she felt running through her veins. Power raced painfully through her, and she fought back the urge to scream.

"Where do you feel it?" Alison asked.

"Near the palace." Carth took small breaths to keep from vomiting. The rolling nausea in her stomach returned again and again. Did that mean that the attackers flickered over and over, or was there another reason she felt this way?

A thunderous explosion filled the air. Alison looked away from her, eyes wide. "That's not *near* the palace. That *was* the palace."

"Come on," Carth said.

"You need to lie down!"

Carth swallowed back the nausea and shook her head. "We need to see what's happening."

She suppressed the urge to vomit again as they raced across the yard. Most of the others they passed went the other way, heading away from the explosion. This was the second time Carth had been foolish enough to race toward an attack, but she had to know if it was the Hjan or the Reshian, as Avera thought.

When they reached the palace, Carth and Alison found that a section along the east wall had caved in, leaving a gaping wound. They stared at it, neither of them able to speak, as people streamed from the palace.

"What happened?" Alison asked finally.

"The Hjan," Carth answered. There was no longer any sense of the same power building, none of the nausea. That had disappeared while they ran, leaving nothing that would tell her that the Hjan remained here, a danger to others. A'ras magic flowed, and she detected the control used by the various practitioners, much more than any student would possess. More than she would be able to manage at this stage in her training. There were masters at work here. Carth would love to see what they were doing, but then she feared getting too close and getting caught.

"If they were able to do this," Alison started, turning to Carth, "how were you able to survive?"

Carth swallowed. How *had* she survived? She'd been lucky that nothing more had happened to her, but then, she had barely survived the attack. Had it not been for the arrival of the masters and their ability to hold him off, she *wouldn't* have survived.

"I got lucky," she said.

Lyanna appeared at the doorway to the palace with Harrison following. They both looked exhausted, and Lyanna had a long gash running along the side of her face. Harrison had his hands clasped in front of him and his eyes studied the grounds, surveying them carefully, as if he expected another attack. From the power he held, and the way he kept his hand near the hilt of his sword, she suspected he did.

"Why would they attack us here?" Alison said.

Carth shook her head. She didn't have the answers. "Invar said the Hjan seek power. That's the reason for the attack. Avera thought another attack was coming, but the other masters thought she was late for what had already happened."

"Avera returned?" Alison asked.

Carth nodded.

"And you saw her?"

"I saw her. She was injured and tired, but otherwise fine."

Alison squeezed her eyes closed and nodded. "Doesn't make sense, though. The palace and these grounds are bound to have A'ras capable of facing an attack. Why risk that? Why any of this?" Alison asked. "Especially with so many here?"

Carth shook her head. "Maybe they wanted to show force," she suggested.

"Or they sought something."

Alison gasped and spun to see Invar standing behind them. Her back straightened and she almost bowed before catching herself.

Invar ignored her, staring at Carth. "Interesting that you were present for both of these attacks, isn't it?"

Carth swallowed. "I heard the attack here on the palace and came to see what happened."

She looked around, thankful that there were others now in the yard outside the palace, including other students. Samis stood a good distance back with his two closest friends, Bardin and Kale. Of them, only Samis looked over at her. His face clouded when he saw Invar with them.

"Heard the attack, not sensed it? Is that not what you told me, Ms. Rel?"

"I sensed it, too, Master Invar," Alison said.

Carth looked to her with relief in her eyes. Alison might not be the tallest of the A'ras students, but she possessed the right amount of feistiness—probably the reason that she and

Carth had become such fast friends.

"I don't know how you *couldn't*," Alison went on. "What caused this? Is it the same thing that attacked earlier?"

Invar looked at Carth through narrowed eyes before turning his attention back to Alison. "Ms. Cantor, I think we can both agree that the attacks were likely the same, as I am sure your friend here would confirm."

Invar watched Carth for a moment, and when she didn't say anything, he only smiled.

"You said the attackers sought something. What would they have wanted in the palace?" Alison asked. Carth shot her a warning glare, wishing her friend would just let it drop, but Alison ignored her. "They wouldn't have attacked the palace if there wasn't something they wanted there, would they? I can't imagine what they would expect to find within the palace, can you, Carth?"

Carth looked at her feet, pointedly trying *not* to notice the way Invar watched her appraisingly. Maybe he hadn't approached her to teach. Maybe it had only been about learning why she had struggled to progress through the A'ras as she had. That had caused some consternation among those who sought to teach her.

"I can't imagine either," she said.

Invar stood in front of her, power radiating from him. She could feel the way he held on to his magic, and tensed up, almost taking a step back. "No? You who have been in a place so few not masters have ever visited cannot think of what they might want?"

Carth looked up and tried not to see the way Alison

stared at her out of the corner of her eye. She didn't want to answer any more questions, but she knew she would have to, especially now, and would need to explain how Invar and Lyanna had led her into the Master Hall. But that would come later.

"They attacked there?"

"What else do you think is at that end of the palace?" Invar asked.

Carth looked over to the palace and realized that would have been true. The attack might have hit the Master Hall. "What did they take?"

A scowl crossed Invar's face. "Take? What kind of masters would we be if we couldn't protect our hall? They reached nothing, Ms. Rel. Three masters remained in the hall, thankfully attending to other duties. Had we not…" He pressed his lips together into a tight line. "Regardless, unlike with the wall, they were not able to breach our hall. What interests me more is what they thought they would find and why they would risk it, knowing there would be masters in the hall."

"What if they weren't after something in the hall?" Carth asked.

"Many seek power, Ms. Rel. These attackers sought to claim the knowledge the A'ras have gained over the centuries, though such knowledge would not help them reach it themselves. It is as much about the technique as it is the practitioner. If they don't select the right person, they cannot use the power in the same way."

Carth wondered if the Hjan had any interest in using the

power the same way the A'ras did, or if they thought to use it for a different purpose. But she also wondered if perhaps chasing power was not the reason for the attack. When the Hjan had attacked before—when they had come for her mother and then tried to collect the children—had that been about power, or was there some other reason? Carth hadn't known, and Jhon hadn't known, and now Felyn was dead, killed by her hand and with magic she still didn't know how to control.

"Was it the Hjan again?" she asked.

Invar didn't answer.

"It felt the same as the last one, but Avera was concerned about the Reshian. Why?"

"As one of the ashai, that is none of your concern, Ms. Rel," Invar said.

What could she say? She wanted to know what had happened, if only because she'd been involved in it. "I…"

"Master Invar."

Carth looked over to see a pair of maroon-sashed A'ras approach Invar. Both wore scarves around their necks, and one of the men had a long curved sword with a black blade hanging from his belt. The other wore a row of knives. Carth hadn't seen either of them before, but Invar seemed to recognize them.

"What is it, Jonah?"

The man with the curved sword took a deep breath as he straightened his back. "Master Harrison asked that you come evaluate the integrity of the wall. We have repaired the breach, but he requests that someone with your ability ensure that it is secure." There was a hint of an edge to Jonah's tone that made Carth wonder if he believed Invar would offer anything that he didn't.

"You may tell Master Harrison that I will visit the breach soon. Keep your men stationed there until I arrive."

"Is that necessary? The breach has been repaired, and there isn't—"

"Repaired, but is it secured?" Invar asked. "The entire wall needs to be evaluated. Such breaches should not have been possible, or do you not remember the lessons I taught you when you were still one of the ashai?"

Jonah nodded curtly and quickly. "I remember them well, Master Invar, which is why I think that you can trust the work I placed."

Invar cocked his head to the side. "I suspect that you do. That doesn't change the fact that I will check them as Master Harrison has requested."

Jonah glanced at Carth. His eyes narrowed and then he hurried away along with the other A'ras. "Now, Ms. Rel," Invar began when they had departed, "I remain curious what you think of the attack."

Carth looked over at the palace, wishing she had something profound to say and feeling completely at a loss. How had the attack even happened in the first place?

"How did they manage to get past the walls and the protections you placed there?" she asked.

"They were placed there by other masters besides only myself, but yes, the protections should have kept them out. The Hjan are one of the reasons such protections exist in the first place." Invar guided them away from the palace, all the while keeping his attention on the building.

Carth could make out the focus in his eyes, and the concern that covered his face. He held on to power the entire time, and it burned within her blood, calling to her. Without meaning to, she allowed some of her magic to seep forward.

"How?" Carth asked.

Invar shook his head. "If this is the Hjan, it would be because they continue to learn new tricks, Ms. Rel, much as we must continue to develop skills. If this is something else…" His frown deepened. "Return to the cosak," he said, as if deciding. "This is not a place for the ashai."

He strode away from them, leaving Carth staring after him. Alison, for one of the rare times, remained silent. After Invar disappeared, she turned to Carth.

"Do you think we're safe here?" she asked.

Carth stared at the missing section of the palace wall. If it was anything like what had happened with the part around the yard, the masters would see it repaired quickly, whether using their magic or employing a fleet of masons.

The question troubled her. As much as it irritated her to remain on the palace grounds, they had always been a place of safety while the ashai studied. Now that safety was gone, torn from them.

"Will they attack again?" Alison asked.

"I don't know."

"Can you tell when they might? You knew when it happened this time, didn't you?"

Carth nodded. "I feel it. That's why I got sick, I think."

"You'll let me know if you feel sick again?"

Carth tried to smile at her reassuringly, but what good would telling Alison do? They weren't talented enough to stop an attack on the grounds. All Carth could do was hide. And if the A'ras magic held, she wouldn't even be able to use the shadows to do it.

"Will you?" Alison pressed.

Carth could only nod.

Chapter 7

Most remained on edge over the next few days. Few spoke about the attack, though those who did looked at Carth a little differently than before. No longer did she hear murmurs about letting the masters take care of an attacker, or boasts that others would have managed to fight off such an attack. Now she heard murmurs of "lucky" and "blessed." The last reminded her too much of what Jhon had claimed of her, and Carth no longer felt that she was shadow blessed.

Invar found her early in the morning on her way to the lecture hall. He wore a sash of maroon around his waist, almost a belt, pulling in his long, flowing shirt. Wrinkles lined the corners of his eyes and his face looked hollowed, as if he hadn't slept much over the last few days.

"We need to talk, Ms. Rel."

Carth looked around, but none of the other students were around. Even Alison hadn't come to her room this morning, something she usually did when the sun first started creeping through the windows.

"What do you want to talk to me about?"

Invar motioned for her to follow. As she glanced once more toward the lecture hall, she saw Alison. Her friend offered her a reassuring smile, but it did nothing to shake the jittery sense she had, the nerves that left her stomach fluttering, at least in a way that was different from what she'd felt when the Hjan had attacked.

"It is time that we speak about the last attack," Invar said as they moved away from the lecture hall. Carth caught a glimpse of Samis and saw him frown as he realized that she walked with Invar. Likely he thought Invar was offering to teach her, which was nearly as bad as some of the other rumors that had been spreading about her.

"The one on the palace?"

Invar glanced over. "The palace. You knew we were attacked."

Carth swallowed. Did Invar think she somehow had something to do with the attack? "I... I sensed something around the same time as the attack," she said carefully.

Invar paused. "What did you sense, Ms. Rel? Is it the same as what you sense with the A'ras?"

Carth wished she had never said anything about what she detected with the A'ras. It did nothing other than draw attention to her, and she wanted nothing more than to hide from attention like that. Especially when it came from the masters.

"It wasn't the same."

"Describe it, please."

It wasn't so much a request as it was a command. "With the A'ras, I feel a... a burning inside when power is used."

He tipped his head toward her. "Do you feel this now?"

Carth shook her head.

"And now?"

The steady sense of A'ras magic used started to build, and she could feel it as it radiated from Invar. He pulled on significant power, leaving Carth's mouth dry, knowing there was nothing she could do to oppose that kind of strength. It was a wonder the Hjan had fared as well as he had against Invar.

She nodded.

"Interesting." The power dissipated. "What do you detect with the Hjan?"

She swallowed again. "With the Hjan, I think it's tied to the flickering. At the wall, when he flickered, I felt it as a rolling nausea. When they attacked the palace, I felt it the same, only much worse."

"There were more attackers," Invar admitted. "And three Hjan, if what I can trace is correct."

By stating it that way, did he imply there were other attackers? "How were they repelled?"

Invar pressed his lips together in a deepening frown. "I am not without capabilities, Ms. Rel."

"I didn't mean—"

He laughed then, disarming her. "I know you didn't mean anything by it. I find it intriguing that you can detect A'ras magic, Ms. Rel."

"But the masters—"

"Most have other ways of detecting magic, but few possess what you describe. You have a unique gift, it would seem."

He motioned her to follow, and she realized that he led her toward the palace. Carth glanced toward the distant sight of the lecture hall, for the first time longing to join the other ashai, knowing that rumors of Invar calling her away were already spreading. There was nothing for her to do but follow.

Invar stopped outside the palace. The light of the early-morning sun shone over the top of the wall, sending streaks of orange and red along the walls. He stood with his hands clasped behind his back, staring at the damaged section of the palace. Stonework had already begun, but it was slow. In spite of that, Carth felt the power emanating from the palace, a surge of power that told her the A'ras masters had placed protections upon the walls.

"What do you sense here, Ms. Rel?"

"You've placed protections on the palace," she answered. She didn't even bother trying to obscure what she could sense. What good would that do her with one of the masters? He'd already discovered enough about what she could do to make it uncomfortable for her.

"Did you notice them before?"

Carth tried to remember what the palace had felt like in the past. What had she noticed? Was there power mixed into the palace itself, or had it only been in the wall surrounding the grounds? "I don't think so," she said.

He started forward, motioning for her to follow. Invar weaved through fallen debris, the scattered and broken fragments of the shattered wall, but there was nothing else here. Only the damage to the structure. Carth hadn't come this close since the attack, not wanting to risk the ire of the masters, but now that she was here, she would have expected to see more than only stone.

"They didn't damage anything other than the structure," she said softly.

Invar studied her. "And why do you think that is?"

Carth touched a section of the stone, letting her fingers run across it. As she did, she recognized the strength and the power that flowed through it, practically humming within. "There was another barrier here," she said. "They peeled away the stone, but that was all they could reach."

"Very good, Ms. Rel. I am impressed that you can pick up so much as only ashai."

Carth didn't know whether she should take the comment as a compliment or whether she should fear that Invar suspected she had another motive. "That's what I detect now, isn't it?"

Invar nodded. "The protection you detect isn't new, but it *was* hidden. The stone had protections of its own, but those were destroyed, much like the protections within the wall were circumvented. They knew about those protections. They didn't know about the additional barrier when they attacked the last time. They will when they come again."

"You expect the Hjan to come again?"

"Them or others. I expect them to continue their attacks until they're successful. Either that or we defeat them."

Carth thought about the way she'd seen the man move, the flickering way he'd appeared and disappeared. If the Hjan could move in such a way, how would the A'ras expect to keep them from the palace? If the magic in the walls and the magic the A'ras had placed inside the palace couldn't do it, what hope did they have?

Invar picked his way through the pile of rock and reached the open section of the wall. Carth followed and stood at his side, peering over the rebuilt section, where she could see into the palace. Masons worked along the wall, hurrying out of the way to give the master space when Invar approached.

"What do you see here?" he asked.

"The palace," she answered quickly.

Invar looked at her, disappointment painting his face. "Yes. The palace. Do you think you can be more specific, Ms. Rel?"

Carth stared into the opening, wondering what Invar wanted her to see. The other side led into a long hallway. Lanterns hung on walls adorned with paintings. Carth had never seen the hall before, but then she had only been in the palace one other time, and that had been to reach the Master Hall. "I don't know. It's different than where you brought me," she said.

"It is. What makes it different?"

She knew he tested her, but didn't know *why*. What did it matter what she saw on this side of the wall? The damage had been done to the palace, and from what Invar said, the masters had managed to protect it.

"You said there were three masters here, and that was how you managed to protect the palace," she said carefully. "Avera, Lyanna, and yourself. But I would have thought you would have been in the Master Hall."

"Why is that important?" he asked.

It wasn't, she didn't think. "This doesn't look like Master Hall is all. The decorations are finer, as is the gilding along the doors, and the gold to the lanterns…" Carth gasped, realizing what she thought Invar intended for her to see. "This is the royal family's quarters, isn't it?"

Invar's face darkened. "You're every bit as observant as I've been led to believe," he said softly. "Yes. This would be the quarters for the Alisant family, the founders of Nyaesh. Had we not placed a separate protective layer, the Hjan would have broken into the palace and would have managed to run free."

"I thought you said they wanted to take something."

"Oh, I think they did want that. We managed to suppress it."

"I don't understand."

Invar motioned for her to follow as he weaved away from the rocks. "It all revolves around the purpose of the Hjan."

"They collect power. Magic."

"That is only a part of what they do, and not all of the Hjan seek that power. Others have a different role."

"Such as?"

Invar turned to her. "They are assassins."

Carth gasped again. "You think the Hjan attacked to kill members of the royal family?"

"I don't know why they broke in, but they subjected themselves to a significant risk coming here. They would have needed to find a way to break through our protections, so coming here risked exposing what they had learned."

"Now that you've stopped them?"

"I don't know that we stopped them at all," Invar said.

"But they didn't get past the barrier!" This close to it, Carth was much more aware of it than she had been when standing even a few feet farther back. With each step away from the palace, the sense of the invisible barrier began to fade, eventually leaving her with little more than a steady tingling beneath her skin.

"They did not, but I question whether they expected to. One attacker came the first time, and we managed to fend him off. He seemed to have little challenge escaping us, almost as if he expected that he wouldn't make it very far onto the palace grounds before he was caught. Then three more attacked. This time, they managed to get quite a bit farther onto the grounds, even penetrating the palace, and escaped before we were able to reach them. If that was their attack, wouldn't they have pressed harder? Would they not have attempted to fight? Yet they did not. They turned as soon as the hidden barrier we'd placed within the palace was exposed."

Carth couldn't take her eyes off the palace as she thought through what Invar had told her. Could the Hjan really be only beginning their attack? "There will be another?"

Invar took a long, slow breath and exhaled in a sigh. "I fear that there will, and that the next time, we won't be prepared for the destruction brought to Nyaesh."

"What about the Reshian?"

Invar waved his hand. "I don't believe the Reshian have as much to do with this as Harrison thinks. They wouldn't side with the Hjan, which is the only explanation that would tie them together."

"Why?"

"That… that is a longer story than I can tell you. Once you climb higher within the A'ras, perhaps then I can share."

"Why are you telling me this?"

Carth could feel the weight of Invar's attention as he studied her, like it was a physical entity that crawled over her, weighing her for a moment and appraising her. She wondered if she passed his inspection.

"I do not think that I would have, but circumstances make me question. You faced the Hjan before joining the ranks of the ashai."

Carth nodded. "A man named Felyn."

"You claim he killed your parents."

"If he didn't, then the A'ras did."

Invar's eyes widened slightly at the comment. "Is that what you think?"

"I know what I saw when my mother died. I spent months believing that the A'ras had killed her, only learning later that it had been Felyn."

"How did you discover that it was Felyn?"

Did she share with him the truth? Avera had likely told the other masters that Jhon had offered her training, and might even have shared with him that she was shadow blessed, but she hadn't discovered how much even Avera knew of how she was shadow born.

"A man helped me."

"A man you knew as Jhon."

Carth nodded. So Invar knew that much. "Do you know him by a different name?"

Invar shrugged. "The name matters little. What matters is what he intends, the man that he is. Why did he help you?"

She hesitated, but this close to the palace, after she had seen the destruction and with Invar watching, she felt as if she had to share as much as possible. Not all. Carth didn't think she could share everything about herself yet, but enough that would explain why Jhon had agreed to work with her. "He learned about my parents, and where I came from."

Invar considered her. "Rel. Carth... short for Carthenne, I imagine?"

She flushed and nodded.

Invar's eyes went closed and he nodded slowly. "You are of Ih-lash, then," he said softly.

"My parents were. I don't remember it."

His eyes opened and he watched her. "Many from Ih-lash receive a certain kind of training. Is that what happened with you?"

Carth swallowed, thinking of what she used to do with her father. "My parents used to play games with me. They would lead me through the city with different tasks. Follow my mother without her seeing me. Find my father when he hid. Things like that. I think those games were his way of teaching me what I needed to know about Ih-lash."

She would never know if her father had known that she was shadow blessed, or if he had suspected. Supposing he hadn't suspected, would he have changed anything if he'd

68

known? Would her parents have taught her any differently, or would it have been the very same as what she'd learned from them?

"Games. Interesting. I admit that I do not know much about the training used by the Ih-lash."

She hesitated. Should she tell him about her connection to the shadows? If she didn't, would he discover anyway?

"There's something else, Master Invar. I... I'm connected to the shadows."

The corners of his eyes twitched slightly. "You are shadow blessed?"

She nodded.

"That should not be possible."

"Why?"

He rubbed his knuckles into the corner of his eyes. "Ah, Jhon, what have you done?" he said under his breath.

"Master Invar?"

He sighed. "What you are taught here is unlike the shadow blessing. That's not to say that one cannot possess both magics, but it would be... unusual. It might explain why you are so easily able to detect A'ras magic, and why you detected the presence of the Hjan."

Carth squeezed her hands together. "Master Invar? I haven't managed to use the shadows since I've been here. It's only been—"

"Since the attack."

Carth nodded.

"When the first Hjan attacked the wall, he disrupted a flow of power that has been layered on the walls for hundreds of years, since the founders of the city came to Nyaesh. Layer after layer, like growth rings on a tree. All of that shattered. Those layers prevent most of the other powers in the world from working on this side of the wall. It is meant to protect us, but also to protect the royal family. The only magic that should exist within the palace grounds is the A'ras magic."

"You're saying that changed with the attack."

"I'm saying they learned a way to destroy generations of magic. That is no small feat, Ms. Rel. And now that they did, we are more prone to another attack." He looked at her askance. "I thought that I might ask you to notify us when you detect the Hjan again"—he tipped his head, and his mouth pinched into a thin line for a long moment—"but perhaps I need to do more than that."

A sinking feeling began to form in Carth's stomach.

"I think it is time that I take on another student. What do you say, Ms. Rel?"

What could she say? The offer should be a great honor. Why, then, did she feel like she was more trapped than ever?

Chapter 8

The lower level of the palace was a dark and dank place, stinking of mold and the wet of earth. Carth heard a steady dripping sound but didn't know if it was real or her imagination. A single lantern flickered in the corner, burning a thick oil that filled the air with another pungent aroma. She didn't know why the flame flickered as it did and preferred not to think about what would cause it to dance in the small room where no wind blew. Her mind created plenty of suggestions as to what might be the cause, such as some creature lurking in the shadows, close enough to pounce on her if she lost her focus.

She stood with her back to the wall, focusing on the A'ras magic as Invar had instructed. Every attempt she made at pulling the magic from herself quickly failed. It didn't *want* to come from her quickly—it never had—and regardless of what tricks and techniques he thought to show her, she wasn't convinced she would be able to do it any better than she usually did.

"You struggle with your focus," he said. It was possibly

the fifth or sixth time he had said the same to her today. Each day had been the same.

"I have always struggled with pulling the A'ras magic from myself," Carth said.

Invar stopped in front of her and crossed his arms. This close to her, he carried a floral scent, a strange smell that reminded her in some ways of her mother. "You use the power well enough when it comes."

Carth nodded. "When it comes. Countless instructors have tried to coax it from me faster, but nothing works. It's just not how I reach it."

"There is something that prevents you from reaching it quickly," Invar said, staring at Carth as if she was some sort of puzzle that he'd like to solve. "The power is there, which tells me that you have the ability, but you do not access it easily."

"It's taken you three days to be able to tell me what I already knew?" Carth immediately regretted snapping at him, but it seemed like Invar didn't listen to her. None of her instructors ever *really* listened to her.

"I try to understand, Ms. Rel, as should you. The key to learning is understanding. I should think that you would be interested in trying to understand so that you can better reach your full potential."

Carth suppressed a frustrated sigh. She had been through this with countless other instructors, and she didn't expect a different result just because she now worked with one of the masters, but she owed it to Invar to at least give him a chance. "I have spent the last five years trying to understand my abilities," Carth said. "As you say, the power is there, and I have managed to use it, but it takes me longer to get it going. It's like it's... *thick*," she said. "The more I use it, the thinner it becomes, and the easier it is for me to draw upon."

That fit with what she felt, even if the explanation made little sense. The magic burned inside her and seemed to flow from within her blood. When she reached for it, she had to pull it out of her blood. Those first attempts took incredible strength and pained her in the process. The more she pulled on it, the easier it became. The problem was, the longer she held on to that power, the more strength it required. Eventually, she ran out of the strength needed to maintain it.

"Thick," Invar said. "I do not believe that I've ever heard the magic described as thick."

He paused as he paced in front of her, the shadows from the single lantern leaving half of his face in darkness. When he'd first brought her to this room, Carth had hoped she might be able to reach the shadows and use her shadow magic, half-hoping that Invar could help with that, but he had made it clear he was only interested in her A'ras potential. The lower-level room, one that was deep beneath the palace, was meant to confine the magic they used and prevent others from noting what she did.

"What's it like when you reach for your potential?" Invar asked.

"I've *told* you what it's like."

"No. You said that it's thick and that it is harder to get going, but once you do, it becomes easier to draw upon. Did that sum up what you have told me?"

73

Carth nodded.

"That explains nothing about what you do, only what you sense."

Carth started pulling on the potential within her, using the focus of the knife that she'd taken from the A'ras, drawing through her blood as she did. As always, power came to her slowly, so that she had to tear it from herself. She held it, letting it flow through her and through the knife so that she could maintain the focus.

"You're holding power now," Invar noted.

"I am." He had said that others didn't detect the use of power the same way she did, but Invar seemed plenty able to note when she prepared to use her magic.

"What did you do to draw it?"

"I… I pulled on the source from within me. It's in my blood, I think, but I have to tear it free. That's what hurts the most."

"Hurts?"

She nodded. That was the part of using the A'ras magic that made her the most miserable. She had to tear it from herself, and when she did, she felt the way it ripped free, like a scab torn from a wound.

"Once you hold it, what do you feel?" he asked.

"I feel… I feel the power as it flows through me," she answered. "Now that I'm holding it, I can use it."

"Show me."

"Show you what?"

"Create a barrier. Do not let me through."

"Master Invar?"

"Don't you think you can do it, Ms. Rel? You have been an ashai for five years. I think this is a fairly straightforward request, do you not?"

She nodded. It *was* an easy enough request, and actually similar to what she used when she sparred, only she wasn't accustomed to simply holding a barrier.

"Now, Ms. Rel."

Carth pulled through herself, drawing on the strength she summoned, that potential that was deep within her, and then curved it out and around her. A sizzling barrier of energy surged, pressing out and away from her until it snapped into focus.

Invar tipped his head. Even with the barrier, Carth was aware of how he used his magic, feeling it as a burning sense that raced through her blood. Invar was a powerful practitioner of the A'ras magic, and the force he drew upon left her mouth dry.

When he took a step forward, he butted up against the barrier.

Then he pushed.

Invar used a combination of magic and sheer strength as he attempted to push past her barrier. Carth held strong, a battle of wills that she refused to lose. The magic flowed through her, and she pulled on more and more, sending the barrier out and out until it pushed Invar back.

Had she not already pulled on her power, she wouldn't have been able to do it. If she had needed to create the connection, she would have been too slow to protect herself, but holding on to it was different and allowed her to use her focus on the magic itself and not the creation of it, or the reaching of her potential.

"Good," Invar said.

Power flooded from him in a heartbeat. It seared through her so quickly that she barely had the time to react. Invar took a step forward, easing past her barrier until he stood directly in front of her, a hard expression on his face.

"You have much strength, Ms. Rel. Are you aware of that?"

"I do all right when I can use the power, but it's the reaching that slows me down."

"I can see that. But once you manage, you have nearly as much strength as the masters I have trained. With time, and with training, you could be quite skilled."

Invar took a step back, and his magic faded. "We will work on your speed. I believe this must be something in your mind, and if we can get past this fear you have of using your magic—"

"I'm not afraid of using it."

"No? If you didn't fear it, you wouldn't have such difficulty drawing upon it when needed. I wonder if it is something about the way your parents taught you to reach the… other… talents you possess." He said that last to himself but watched her as he said it. "Tomorrow, we will meet at the palace gate. I believe you know how to find it?"

Carth flushed, realizing that Invar must have been watching her longer than she had realized. That was the only way he would know that she went to the palace gates, and that she checked them to see if they were locked, always hoping that one day she would find them open and would catch a glimpse of the city on the other side. Eventually, she knew, she would be granted the ability to leave, but that day seemed impossibly far away.

"I know how to find it."

Invar turned toward the door. "Now, you will practice reaching your potential. I will come for you when it is time for you to depart."

Carth sat at a table in the dining hall, her mind feeling like she'd spent the night drinking ale. All she wanted was sleep, but first she needed food. Exhaustion threatened to topple her over where she sat, and she fought to remain upright in the chair.

Alison sat across from her, slowly chewing the crisp carrot she held up to her face. "Why does he take you into the basement of the palace?" she asked between bites.

Carth shook her head. "I think he intends for me to learn there," she answered. "It's his practice room."

Alison took another bite of the carrot and chewed slowly, making a face as she did. "What kind of things does he have you learning? Most think that you're already moving past what you need to know to pass out of the ashai."

Carth snorted. "I'm practicing reaching my potential. Over and over and over and—"

"That's it? That's the sort of thing you learn when you first come to the palace! Why would he have you practicing that?"

Carth pushed her lump of stale bread through the gravy on her plate and took a bite. The food didn't even taste good today, she was so tired. What she needed was to sleep, maybe for the next two days, but unfortunately she would be going with Invar again tomorrow, and the next day, and the one after that...

She should have refused him, but if she thought the whispers about her were bad now, what would they have been like if the others found out that she had refused to learn from one of the masters?

"That's all I've been learning," Carth said.

"I'm sorry," Alison said with a whisper. "Don't tell others, though. They all think Invar is showing you some of his complicated magic, and training you to follow him as master. It might be better to let them keep believing."

Carth doubted that would ever be the case. She could barely reach her magic fast enough, let alone do anything more with it, and certainly nothing like what Invar could do. When she held on to her magic, she managed to push him back, but there needed to be more to it than that.

"Let them think whatever they want," she said, pushing the rest of her bread into her mouth. She stood and carried her tray to the kitchen, rinsing it as was expected of the ashai. One of the other students—a slightly older boy named Marten—was in the kitchen and glanced over as she entered, a half smile on his face. Carth ignored him.

Alison trailed after her as she departed the kitchen, saying nothing but giving her space. When Carth stepped out of the dining hall, a trio of boys stood waiting. Two were

Samis's friends, Bardin and Kale, both with the same swath of dark hair and the high cheeks that marked them of Nyaesh birth. The third was Landon, an older boy who would be fully A'ras whenever he passed the test. Carth always thought he had a certain arrogance about him that came from being distantly descended from the ruling family. From what she'd learned, he had been raised within the palace walls. All three carried short swords and rested their hands on the hilts.

Fatigue or the food had made her nauseous, and she tried turning away from them.

"What is this?" Alison demanded, stepping in front of them and blocking Carth from confronting them. As tired as she was, she didn't think she had the strength to deal with them.

"Right of spar," Landon said.

"That's not fair. You can't do that after we've just eaten," Alison said.

He shook his head. Unlike the other two boys, he had blond hair and was muscular, standing nearly a foot taller than Carth. Whereas most found Samis attractive, his muscular build matching his symmetrical face and easy smile, Landon had a long, hooked nose, and his hair hung straight—almost limp—to his shoulders.

"There's always the right of sparring. I claim the right."

"As do I," Bardin and Kale both said, almost in unison.

"Fine. Let me get this over with," Alison muttered.

Landon scowled at her. "Not you. Where's the challenge in that? Her," he said, motioning to Carth.

Carth hadn't expected them to come for Alison. She might be a reasonably gifted student, but there were many who knew that she chose to ignore the tradition of sparring, and often flat-out refused if challenged.

"You can't think you'll face Carth after what she's been through, can you?" she asked, watching Carth as she said it. As tired as she was, Carth didn't think she'd have the strength to even lift the knife, let alone use it to focus her potential as she pulled on the magic.

"The right of sparring sets no limits, much like the A'ras cannot have any limits," Landon said.

"You've been spending too much time in Kellen's classes," Alison said.

Landon's scowl deepened. "Are you going to step aside, or am I going to have to—"

Alison let out a frustrated sigh. "Fine. If you're going to pull this shit with Carth, then I challenge *you* with the right of sparring."

Landon slowly pulled his gaze away from Carth and fixed Alison with a look that bordered on amusement. "You challenge *me*? Is that really what you want to do, Cantor?"

Alison stepped closer to Landon and pulled her pair of knives from sheaths at her waist. Carth had rarely seen her use her knives and doubted that Alison was as skilled with them as Landon was, but he at least eyed them carefully. "Does that make you nervous?" She twisted one of the knives so that she could jab it toward Bardin. "What about you? Think you want to try your luck?"

Landon tried to look past Alison, but she kept pressing

toward him, forcing him to focus on her, even when he obviously thought he would be given a chance to contest Carth. "We'll do this, Cantor, but tomorrow. Don't think to try to slink off and hide."

Alison flourished her knives before slipping them back into the sheaths at her waist. "I'll be there. I expect you'll change your mind tomorrow, though."

Landon's scowl deepened, and he motioned to Kale and Bardin, leading them away. When they were gone, Alison let out a long sigh. "Well, that should be interesting."

"Thanks. You don't have to do that."

Alison grinned. "Don't worry, I don't think I will." She started off without explaining what she meant. "Besides, I didn't want you having to deal with them after a day like you had today. I can see how wiped you are. Landon and the other two only wanted to challenge you because you're working with Invar. It's like they think they can impress him by facing you."

"That's not going to impress Invar."

Alison shrugged. "Probably not. That doesn't change the fact that they think it will." They stopped at the cosak, and Alison gave her a quick hug. "Get some rest. I'll deal with them and you can worry about what you need to do to make Invar happy tomorrow. Hopefully it will be more than simply showing him how you reach your potential."

"That's probably all he'll have me do again. That's all he's had me doing since he started working with me." Except she knew that tomorrow would be different, if only because he wanted her to meet him at the palace gate. Maybe he thought to show her how he placed the protections on the walls. She didn't dare think about the other possibility—that she might actually get to leave the palace grounds.

Chapter 9

"You seem surprised, Ms. Rel," Invar said. He walked about three paces in front of her, the wide maroon sash of the A'ras wrapped around his wrist, leaving him otherwise covered in a plain brown robe that dragged across the ground.

Carth kept her eyes sweeping the streets around her, her hand clasping the stone coin Invar had given her, a key of sorts to leaving the palace. It had been years since she'd left and the shock of the city caught her off guard. She didn't remember how dirty the streets were, or the way the buildings on either side seemed to loom toward the street, some rising high enough to block out the sunlight.

Through it all, she felt the soft, tickling awareness of the shadows.

Carth wanted to reach for them, use them to cloak herself, but she didn't dare, not while Invar remained nearby, watching. Instead, she kept herself content letting the sense of the shadows play across the back of her mind, feeling something like a gentle caress.

She should not. The shadows distracted her from the

A'ras magic, and that was what Invar wanted her to focus on.

"It's been some time since I left the grounds," she said.

Invar waved with his free hand. Carth noted that the other remained on the hilt of his sword. "The ashai must remain on the grounds during their studies. It is… safest that way."

The streets teemed with activity. People bustled past her, many dressed in the simple dark browns and blacks favored by those within Nyaesh. A few wore wide-brimmed hats that shaded their eyes or wraps that covered their heads, leaving only their eyes exposed. With so many different styles of dress, she didn't know how she'd pick out the Hjan, and she thought that was the entire reason Invar had brought her out into the city.

"Why? Why is it safest? The A'ras patrol the streets of Nyaesh. Shouldn't the ashai learn how so that when we pass through, we can help?"

Invar glanced back to her, a serious expression on his face. "There are other threats beyond the Hjan. The Reshian continue to press. They might not have entered the city, but that doesn't mean they will not continue to try. It would be dangerous for an untrained ashai to encounter the Reshian."

Carth chased after him as he disappeared around a corner, turning down an alleyway. As she followed, she remembered how she'd raced through the streets in the months after losing her parents, how she'd discovered that the games her parents had taught her lent her an advantage when it came to collecting scraps. Back then, the streets had become a place to play, a place where she worried about nothing more than avoiding the attention of the A'ras, or of the guild, but even that had been because she hadn't known better. The threats within Nyaesh were greater than she had realized at that time.

Invar stopped when the street started to slope down toward the river. The street was wider here, one of the main thoroughfares stretching between the docks and the rest of the city, letting more of the bright sunlight fill the streets. The noise and commotion from people in the street doubled, leaving little space to move freely. How had she managed to run through here?

"I understand that you know this part of the city," Invar said.

Carth stood at the corner of a bakery, a butcher across the way. The scents from the bakery tickled her nose, and once would have set her mouth watering, but she ate well studying with the A'ras, never quite as hungry as she'd been when running the streets. Even then, Vera had treated her well, ensuring that she wasn't *really* hungry.

"When my parents died, an innkeep took me in."

"She did more than that, from what I understand."

"What is that supposed to mean?"

"It means, Ms. Rel, that she kept you alive. Your parents were targeted, were they not?"

She wrapped her arms around herself, trying not to have flashbacks to the day she'd lost them. While studying within the grounds of the palace, it was easier to forget about what had happened, easier to close off those memories and focus on the reason she studied, trying to hone her magic so that it came more easily to her. But wasn't the reason she studied with the A'ras so that she could find those responsible for her parents' death?

"They were targeted, yes. Felyn killed them."

"Felyn. One of the Hjan, at a time when we did not understand their danger. Impressive that you were able to evade him."

"You knew him?"

As Invar shook his head, his hand squeezed the hilt of his sword, his knuckles going white. "I did not know the man. As much as we might insulate ourselves within Nyaesh—and make no mistake, Ms. Rel, we *are* insulated—much comes to us. I had heard of deadly assassins for years before he ever reached the borders of our city. When Felyn first crossed through, we detected his presence."

"That's why there had been so many patrols," she realized.

Invar nodded. "Observant. Yes, the A'ras had not patrolled the city as much prior to that. We are not soldiers, but we can provide a different kind of protection. When the Hjan reached the city, and when we detected the first presence, there were a few of us who recognized the need to step up our involvement. And when the Hjan left, the Reshian followed." He glanced at her, holding her eyes a moment. "Most fear them related, but those who know understand they were not."

Carth hadn't been in the city long when the patrols had begun. She remembered them well, the sense of brutality from the A'ras, the power she had detected from them even then, and the way people cowered from them. It made sense for people to have been frightened. They weren't accustomed to the A'ras presence, not so openly within the city.

"Why have the A'ras continued patrols, then?" Carth asked.

"You have witnessed the reason, Ms. Rel."

"The Hjan?"

"The Hjan still come to Nyaesh from time to time but have not attacked openly. Not until recently. Always before, we knew they were here. The protections we placed upon the city allow us to know that much, but not much else. When we have fought the Hjan, we have died. The only person known to have stopped one stands next to me. Still, that is not the reason we patrol."

"The Reshian?"

When Invar nodded, she thought back to what she knew of them, which wasn't much, but she would not have expected to need the A'ras to defend against them.

"Most fear the Reshian more than any other attack," he said.

"But not you."

He offered a half-smile. "I fear something else. When Avera witnessed you using A'ras magic against one of the Hjan, all hesitation about your entrance to the ashai faded. You have potential, though it is slow for you. Most imagined that was because you came to us as an older student. Many have learned to reach their potential easily by the time they are your age, which is why I wonder if the games your parents played with you, the skills they thought to teach you, prevented you from reaching it."

Jhon had warned her against sharing that she hadn't used A'ras magic to stop Felyn. She might have used the A'ras knife she had stolen from the fallen man, but it had been shadows that killed him, not A'ras magic.

"I saw you face the Hjan," she said. "I saw how the three of you handled him."

Invar chuckled. "Handled. I think that we did less than handle, though any praise when it comes to the Hjan is appreciated. We managed to hold him off, but still he escaped, much as they do every time we face them. We need to capture one of the Hjan so that we can determine what they target in the city."

"That's why you brought me out here with you?" she asked. "You want to see if I can detect where they might be?"

Invar took a step toward her and leaned in so that his face was barely a hand's width away. "I think you can, Carthenne Rel. And we need that ability of yours if we are to find a way to stop them." He took a deep breath and stepped back. "You have seen what they can do, Ms. Rel. You have seen the way they are willing to attack us. We must find a way to discover them before they attack again."

"What makes you think they'll attack again?"

"They are after something, Ms. Rel. The others might not believe, but I do. Worse, I do not know what they seek, but I fear that even the A'ras will not be strong enough to stop them."

Invar led her through the city for much of the day. He would pause at times and ask her to focus on reaching her potential, and once she did, she had to hold on to it as they made a steady circuit through the city. A few times, they caught a glimpse of some of the other A'ras patrols, but each time, Invar made a point of directing her in a different direction. Once, she thought she saw Samis with one of the patrols, but they didn't get close enough for her to know. It would be better for her to see Samis than Landon, she decided.

The longer she held on to the magic flowing through her, the more tired she became. Her mind rebelled against some of the lessons Invar had for her, things such as creating barriers, or using her power to enhance her speed. All of those were lessons that some of the earliest students were asked, and here one of the masters had her repeating them.

As the day grew longer, shadows began to stretch over the city, filling the streets with undulating pools of darkness. To her, it was more than darkness—it was a sense of power that she had only to reach for. Carth resisted, but the more tired she became, the harder it was to withstand the draw.

"When will we return to the palace?" she asked as they stopped. They were on the edge of the city, standing in the shadows of the massive city wall. Soldiers patrolled along the wall, but there was the occasional flash of maroon telling her they didn't patrol alone.

"You have not left the confines of the grounds in years and now you would return? I am disappointed, Ms. Rel. I thought you would be more interested in spending time out in the city."

"I was. Am. I'm tired."

"For you to gain control of your abilities, you will need to move past the fatigue you feel when using your potential."

"You've had me holding on to my power constantly. You don't do that."

He quirked a brow at her, and a half smile crossed his face. "You are so certain?"

Carth sighed. "I told you I can feel when you use your magic. You're not holding it now."

A sudden smack sent her sliding into the wall. Invar hadn't moved, and as far as she could tell, he hadn't drawn on his magic either. "Are you so certain that I'm not?"

Her heart hammered. She'd been so accustomed to knowing when the A'ras used their magic that she hadn't considered that some would be able to do it without her knowing. If any could, it would be one of the masters. "What? How?"

She was too tired and could barely think straight.

"Nothing more than a trickle. Speed is important, as you've seen, Ms. Rel. When it comes to these attacks, even I must be ready."

A trickle. She'd been holding on to more than that, but then, she had no choice but to hold on to more than a trickle. But how had she not noticed?

Was it a test?

Carth watched Invar, trying to glean something from his neutral expression. Could he have wanted to see what she would do, and whether she would be able to detect him using his magic? Was that another reason he'd brought her with him into the city?

The hours spent using her power left her drained, and she'd only been able to focus on how tired she felt, not bothering to spend any energy thinking about whether there was even a subtle shift of power. It was possible that having her hold on to her magic made it harder for her to detect him.

As she tried to focus on whether she could detect him using his magic even while she was tired, a different sensation came to her, one that made her stomach roll. It was a queasy, greasy feeling and she covered her mouth to try and keep from vomiting.

"They're here," she said.

"You don't look well, Ms. Rel."

"Hjan. They're here."

Power surged from Invar. "Can you identify where?"

She could tell the direction of the power, but she couldn't tell how far away they were. "North."

Invar started off. "Come, Ms. Rel. I will need your... nose? Whatever it is that allows you to detect them."

Carth struggled to keep up with Invar as they weaved between rows of houses, hurrying along streets, making their way deeper into the city. The streets here became familiar, and it took Carth a moment to realize why; this was where she had lived, however briefly.

The nausea flipped in her stomach again. They were close.

Carth pointed, barely able to see clearly, but she didn't need to see to know that this was the last home she'd had. The sounds along the street—even the smells—were the same. Why would the Hjan have come here?

Invar surged power again, unsheathing his sword as he did.

"The shadow blessed."

The voice grated against her ears, ripping through her as the man strode from her old home. "You have returned home, it seems."

Invar jumped forward, sword swinging with deadly A'ras magic.

The Hjan flicked his hand toward him and Invar collapsed.

It was as simple and terrifying as that. Invar didn't move, and Carth didn't know if he even still breathed, now sprawled across the stones outside her family home.

The Hjan turned to face her, eyes burning with a dark intensity. "You intrigue me, shadow blessed. There are not many who manage to do so these days."

Carth reached for her knife, trying to focus her magic as she did, but it came too slowly.

The Hjan stopped in front of her, holding a pair of knives. "There are not many of your kind who remain, did you know that? I have personally seen to nearly a dozen. The rest... they will fall soon enough."

Carth trembled, trying to push magic through the knife, but the connection was difficult. As tired as she was, she couldn't reach her magic as she needed. Even were she not tired, she didn't know if she would be able to reach the magic strongly enough to hold off the Hjan. If Invar fell so easily before him, what could she do?

"Perhaps I will bring you with me to Venass. There are many who would appreciate the opportunity to study one of the shadow blessed."

Through the pain, she felt strength come to her, almost willed into her, the shadows filling her as they had all those years ago.

She *was* shadow blessed. Though she didn't know what that meant for her, she could use those shadows now.

Unable to access her A'ras magic, she reached for the shadows and sent their power through her knife. The Hjan hesitated, flickering a moment as he moved toward her. Wrapped in the shadows as she was, she didn't feel the same twisting nausea she'd felt before.

"You cannot hide from me for long, shadow blessed," he taunted.

He made a movement with his hand, twisting the knives in such a way that light radiated from them and pushed against the shadows. Carth had been out of practice using them and suspected that, had she not been stuck behind the walls of the palace for all those years, she would have better learned how to use them. But now, when she wanted the control, it began to slip from her, slowly pushed away, as if it were too slippery for her to maintain.

Carth took a deep breath, ducking toward the wall of her old house. The shadows were thicker there and pulling on them was easier, letting her practically breathe them in.

The Hjan spun toward her, the light flowing from him.

Carth wouldn't be able to hold on to the shadows for much longer, not like this.

With another breath, she sent the shadows flowing through the knife. Somehow, it seemed to mix with the A'ras magic she still managed to hold, so that when she jumped toward the Hjan, slicing with the knife, she managed to cut him on the arm.

Carth hit the ground hard and lost her breath.

She rolled to the side, scrambling to reach more shadows, but there was no need.

The Hjan had fallen, his breaths coming in strangled gasps, his hand tearing at the arm she'd cut. Carth didn't move any closer, afraid to get too near the fallen Hjan. She watched with horrid fascination as he stabbed at his arm, digging into the flesh with one of his knives. Light flashed from it, blindingly bright.

Carth had to look away. When she turned back, he was gone.

Chapter 10

Carrying Invar back to the palace took all the strength Carth had left. She reached the gate, her arm slipped behind Invar, and only because of the maroon sash around his arm did the doors open. A pair of A'ras met her on the other side, and both quickly grabbed Invar.

"What happened to Master Invar?" Trista asked. She was a lean woman with curly black hair who always seemed to thrust her chest forward as she walked, with far too much stiffness to her back, but Carth had seen her fight and knew she was as skilled with the staff she carried as any of the swordsmen were with their blades.

"An attack."

"I can see that, Ashai Rel. What happened? How were you attacked?"

Carth wondered how much she should be sharing with them and how much she needed to save for the masters. This didn't seem something that Invar would openly share. "I need to find Master Lyanna," she said.

"Master Lyanna is off the grounds," Trista answered.

"What about Avera?"

Trista glanced at the other of the A'ras, a compact man with a pocked face and a thin line for a beard around his chin. "Avera has been gone for—"

"She has not been gone. I saw her all of a few weeks ago," Carth said.

She shouldn't be so curt with the A'ras, especially as she was barely ashai, but exhaustion from working with Invar all day—and then the attack at the end of the day—left her with no patience for niceties.

"We can take you to Master Harrison," the other A'ras said. He had a thick voice, one that sounded like he'd spent the day screaming while she'd spent it trying to use her magic.

Harrison. Of all the masters, she cared for him the least. Whenever he decided to come and teach the students, he always did so with an air of condescension, much like he'd had when Carth had come with news of the attack on the city. Even with Invar, Lyanna, and Erind present for the attack, Harrison still made a point of treating her as if she had fabricated much of it.

"Fine. Harrison is fine, but Invar needs help," she snapped. "Stop delaying and bring him to the palace."

Carth started toward the palace, not bothering to watch whether they followed. When she reached the outer entrance, she paused, waiting for the other two to catch up, knocking at the door as she did.

The massive doors to the palace swung open and Carth hurried in. The A'ras standing guard at the door only shook his head when she entered. Now that she'd been studying with Invar, she came to the palace often enough that he recognized her. She started down the hall that led toward the Master Hall without waiting for the others. Now that they had reached the palace, she knew that they would follow.

"Ms. Rel…"

She froze at the weak voice, turning carefully.

Invar's eyes were open and he looked at her. The two A'ras carrying him both helped to prop him up, but he managed to hold on to enough strength that he was able to assist. The smaller man looked to Trista for guidance and she shrugged.

"I think I can manage now that we're here," Invar said, strength quickly returning. "Especially with Ms. Rel's assistance."

"Carth," Trista said softly. "It appears that Master Invar no longer requires our assistance."

Carth hurried back to him and took Trista's place, with Invar leaning on her. The master was old and looked frail, but he weighed more than she'd expected when she had first started carrying him back to the palace. After all the effort she'd expended just getting him back here, she barely had the strength to keep him upright.

"Master Invar…"

"I can help this time," Invar said. He straightened somewhat and took some of the effort onto himself .

After Trista and the other A'ras left, he pulled on a surge of power that allowed him to stand up with more strength than Carth would have expected. She took a step away from him, thinking that he didn't need her help anymore, but he clasped a hand on her arm to prevent her from getting too far.

"Are you hurt?" Carth asked as they made their way down the corridor to the Master Hall. Carth had been here only twice, but she could trace the steps in her mind.

Invar took a deep breath and with each step, he seemed stronger than the one before. "Less than I should be, I think," he said.

"What do you mean?"

Invar paused at the entrance to the Master Hall, his hand resting on the door. He surged power through it with more strength than Carth could imagine using after everything she'd done during the day. The door swung open and he nodded for her to continue helping him in.

None of the other masters were here. The lantern she'd seen when she had come before remained burning.

She stopped in front of the lantern, holding her hands out in front of it, but found that it wasn't nearly as warm as she would have expected.

"Ms. Rel," Invar said.

She shook herself and turned to help him as he took a seat in one of the chairs. "I'm sorry. The lantern…"

He gave her a quizzical expression. "You really are perceptive, aren't you?"

"What do you mean?"

He shook his head. "Perhaps it is nothing. Tell me," he said, settling his hands on his thighs and leaning slightly forward, "how is it that I still live?"

"The Hjan attacked."

"I am aware that the Hjan attacked," Invar said. "I seem to recall that I was there, however briefly that might have been." He tried to smile, but it failed.

It was only then that Carth realized how exhausted *he* was. Here she'd thought that he managed more strength than she did, marveling at how he used his power to prop himself up and to send the necessary surge of power through the door to open it. But he had used all of his remaining strength to open the door, she suspected. The sense of him pulling on his magic faded, and the feeling of it burning through her disappeared with it.

"What I do not understand—but would like to—is how I am still here."

"I don't know," Carth said.

"Don't know, or don't wish to share?" Invar sighed and leaned back in the chair, letting his eyes fall closed. "I have faced the Hjan several times before, Ms. Rel. There has never been a time when I felt quite so unprepared. They continue to develop new techniques, I fear."

"What happened?"

Invar sighed. "He extinguished the magic burning within me, Ms. Rel."

"I don't understand."

"You are not yet fully A'ras."

"What does that have to do with anything?"

Invar opened his eyes. "It has to do with everything, especially when it comes to the Hjan." He settled himself in the chair, shifting side to side until he was comfortable. "What I will tell you is normally only shared with the A'ras, but seeing as how you saved me, and how you seem to find yourself around the Hjan more often than most, I think it is prudent that you know more about what you face." His gaze drifted toward the massive lantern burning in the center of the room. "When you call upon A'ras magic, what does it feel like?"

Carth frowned. Was this another lesson? If it was, the timing seemed strange, especially with what they had both gone through. "I've told you what it feels like," she said.

"No. You have told me what it is like when you call on the magic, but what does it *feel* like?"

"Fire," she answered immediately. That had always been the case, from the very beginning of her awareness of the A'ras magic. It had always felt like fire to her. First when she detected it, and then when she began to use it.

"Interesting description, Ms. Rel, and I am not sure others would describe it in the same way." He started to smile and shook his head. "To some, it would seem like heat, or warmth."

"How is that different from fire?"

"Place your hand in a hearth and tell me how they are different. They are part of the same spectrum, but they are not the same. Not for most, at least."

He leaned back and didn't say anything for a while. "What is it like when *you* use your magic?" Carth asked.

"Fire," Invar said softly. "Which was why, when he extinguished it, I thought myself dead. Yet I am not, thanks to an ashai."

"I don't know what I did," she said.

"I do not think that likely. I thank you for whatever you did nonetheless."

Carth thought of how she'd used the shadows, how she'd felt the shadows surging through her, filling her. Only through the strength given her by the shadows had she managed to carry Invar back to the palace, but as soon as she'd crossed the palace walls, that connection had faded, disappearing completely.

"What happened to the Hjan?" Invar asked. "Did you kill him?"

She shook her head. "He escaped."

Somehow, she had used the shadows as she'd attacked the Hjan. She had nearly killed him—she realized that now—but he had used the light he'd managed to summon with his knives to burn away the shadows she'd used against him.

"A shame. I think I would have preferred him dead."

"He's the same man who attacked the wall," Carth said.

"I thought as much." He fell silent for a moment before opening his eyes again and fixing her with the intense stare. "The house where we found him. You knew it, didn't you?"

"I knew it."

"It was your home?"

She swallowed. "The last home I had," she said. "Before... before Felyn killed my parents."

"What would compel him to visit that place?"

"I don't know. Another family lives there—at least they did within months of my parents' deaths."

"That is the way of things in Nyaesh," Invar said.

"Everywhere, I suppose, but Nyaesh especially. There is a shortage of homes, and when they become available, whether by tragedy or other means, there are plenty of others waiting to move in. After he attacked where you were found twice, it does make me wonder whether he went to *your* old home thinking to find out something about you."

"There's nothing about me he would want to know."

Invar tipped his head and a hint of a smile played across his lips. "No? Perhaps he would like to know the same thing I would like to know—how an untrained ashai managed to withstand an attack from the Hjan not once, not twice, but three times."

Carth turned her attention to the flame burning in the lantern, losing herself in the way it danced and flickered. "I didn't withstand anything," she said. "I got lucky."

Invar leaned back and let out a sigh. "One time would be luck. Twice even. Three times tells me there is something about you that I don't fully understand. Not only can you detect A'ras magic with more sensitivity than most within these walls, but you were able to tell when one of the Hjan appeared, something not even the masters can manage without expending significant power." He breathed out. "I think that I will need to study you longer, Ms. Rel. For now, I would like to rest."

His breathing slowed and became regular as he fell into a slumber. Carth watched him for a moment, then started from the hall. The lantern caught her attention and she turned to it, staring into the flames.

Invar had asked her what the magic felt like for her, and

she'd described it as fire. For her, it *was* fire. Could others really detect it as warmth and heat? That sounded almost… pleasant. Nothing like the pain she experienced when she detected the magic.

Carth reached toward the flame, holding her hand out to it. There was warmth to it, and she wasn't able to get her hand very close without feeling it grow too hot. It pulled on something inside her that reminded her of when magic flowed, not only from within her, but also when others used their magic.

Invar shifted in his sleep and Carth turned, mistakenly grabbing for the lantern as she did.

She jerked her hand up so that she didn't touch the lantern, but as she did, her hand passed through the flame. Carth sucked in a breath as she pulled her hand back, looking to see if she'd disturbed Invar, but the master remained asleep.

Clutching her hand in her cloak, she ran toward the door. Pain throbbed through her. She wanted nothing more than to scream, but she'd have to do it outside. She didn't want to explain to Invar what had happened.

After everything that had happened today, after surviving an attack from one of the Hjan, she'd get injured *this* way?

Carth felt like a fool.

Worse, as she started from the room, Invar muttered something in his sleep, and she could have sworn she'd heard him say her name, and something about the shadows.

Carth hurried from the hall, and as she did, the pain in her hand throbbed in time with what she remembered of the flame. She tried not to think about it as she made her way back to the cosak and, hopefully, to find sleep.

Chapter 11

Food called to her before sleep. Carth reached the dining hall and found it sparsely populated, which, given the throbbing in her hand, which she'd wrapped with her maroon sash, was probably the best thing. Her stomach rumbled and she hurried to the kitchen to grab a tray, stacking bread onto her tray and scooping stew into a bowl. When she returned to the dining hall, it was no longer empty.

Landon sat at one of the tables and eyed her as soon as she entered. She made her way toward the back of the dining hall, not wanting to deal with him, and sat. The sooner she managed to eat, the sooner she would be able to get back to her room and sleep.

The throbbing in her hand forced her to use the other, and she kept her injured hand under the table as she ate. She dipped the bread into the stew and chewed quickly, ignoring the fact that it had cooled, leaving fat congealing on the surface.

A shadow passed in front of her and she almost tried reaching for it. "What happened to you?" Landon asked, throwing himself onto the chair opposite her.

"Nothing happened."

"I saw how you wrapped your hand. You were out with Master Invar today. What happened?"

Carth looked up from her tray, debating what to share with him, if anything. Landon didn't need to know what had happened and would likely only spread gossip about her, if that wasn't happening already, especially after the way she'd forced herself back onto the grounds.

"I was out with Invar. There was another attack."

Landon's brow furrowed. "An attack? We didn't hear anything about it while I was on patrol."

"You probably wouldn't have," Carth agreed.

Landon set his hands on the table and leaned back. "What kind of attack? No one is stupid enough to risk attacking one of the A'ras masters in the middle of Nyaesh."

"The Hjan are," Carth said. Had she only been faster, she might have managed to stop it, but instead, she'd delayed, thinking he was gone when he wasn't. Now the Hjan still lived and likely would return, better prepared to face her the next time. Without any way to practice using the shadows, Carth worried about what would happen to her with the next attack.

Everything they'd seen so far told her there would be another.

Invar seemed to know more than he shared with her, and she wondered what more he knew about why the Hjan risked attacking in Nyaesh. They couldn't expect to defeat *all* of the A'ras, could they?

"Master Harrison claims the Hjan aren't the real threat."

Carth frowned. "You heard him say that?" she demanded.

Landon met her eyes and shook his head slightly. "I didn't, but Olar did."

Olar was one of the A'ras she'd seen with Landon when they patrolled, and he might actually have enough access to Harrison to make the claim believable. And hadn't Invar implied the same thing? "What does Harrison think attacked the palace, then? What about the wall?"

Landon shrugged. "I can't say I understand the masters well enough to answer, Rel. But if Harrison doesn't think they're much of a threat—"

Carth took a bite and stood. "Not much of a threat? Invar nearly died today because of a single Hjan. If they can face three masters and still escape, what do you think will happen when your *patrol* happens across one? Do you think you'll be lucky enough to succeed where one of the masters couldn't?"

Landon started laughing, and Carth slammed her tray down, sending stew slopping onto his shirt. He casually wiped it away, smearing his finger through it and licking it. "You expect me to believe that Invar nearly died and you somehow only came away with an injured hand? Damn, Rel, I thought you were strange before…"

Carth stormed away, not willing to listen to him taunt her anymore.

She reached her room in the cosak without finding anyone else and jumped into her bed, curling her arms around her legs as she tried to get comfortable enough to sleep. Landon had her on edge, and she struggled to find sleep, memories of the attack rushing through her.

How *had* she managed to stop the Hjan? Not only once, but a second time as well? It was more than being shadow blessed, wasn't it? When Jhon had explained what it meant for her to be shadow blessed, he had mentioned that she had the ability to use the shadows to hide, but what she'd done today, and what she'd done when Felyn had attacked, was more than that. During that first attack, Avera had claimed she'd used A'ras magic, if unintentionally, and Jhon had seemed perfectly content with that answer, but Carth no longer thought it true. She had somehow used the shadow magic, not A'ras magic. And the Hjan hadn't been able to counter it.

Carth sat up, her mind racing. She needed answers, but there was no one here she could ask, not safely. If Invar even suspected she could do more than use the shadows to hide, would he continue to work with her? Would he continue to allow her to study with the A'ras? She didn't know what she wanted, but she didn't want to lose another home.

What else could she do?

Understanding the shadows couldn't happen within the walls of the palace. With the magic used in the walls, there was no way she could reach the shadows strongly enough to understand them, but that meant she had to leave the grounds. She had the token Invar had given her, but if she used it without his permission...

She could always claim that she did it to search for the Hjan so that the next time, they would be better prepared.

Invar might not fully believe it, but the idea wasn't so far off from what he'd asked of her.

It was late in the day and she needed rest, but her mind raced. Besides, what better time for her to understand the shadows than at night, when she would find them everywhere?

Grabbing the A'ras knife she'd had ever since the day her mother died, she slipped it into a sheath on her waist so it would be easier to reach. Next, she swapped the maroon sash wrapped around her hand for a strip of white cotton torn from one of her old dresses and stuffed the sash into a pocket.

Making her way through the cosak and out onto the lawn, she encountered Alison.

"Carth?" Alison asked.

She raised a finger to her lips.

"What are you doing? I heard you were with Invar all day. Rumor has it he was injured and you somehow carried him back to the palace by yourself."

Carth suspected she knew the source of that rumor. She should have known better than to share with Landon what had happened. "We were attacked," Carth whispered.

Alison whistled softly. "I thought Trista was making things up when she said you snapped at her."

Carth smiled to herself. "I might have been a little harsher than I should have been with her."

"She said you commanded her and Heran to carry him to the palace."

"I was getting tired."

Alison laughed and cupped her hand over her mouth. "Did you really say that to her?"

Carth shrugged. "Invar nearly died. I didn't want them dallying."

"Died? What happened? I thought he was working on teaching you to reach your magic more quickly!"

Carth told her about the attack, and how Invar had wanted to use her to detect the presence of the Hjan. She didn't share with her what she suspected about her ability to use the shadows. That wasn't something she wanted to share with anyone until she knew what it meant. Alison might know she was shadow blessed, even if she didn't understand, but something more was happening.

"Where are you going now?" Alison asked. "Master Invar should be too tired to work with you if what you said is true."

"I..." Carth hesitated. Alison was her closest friend, and she hated the idea of keeping things from her, but she didn't know what to make of what she'd done with the shadows. What would Alison think if Carth admitted to using shadows and sending them through the knife rather than A'ras magic, or told her that the shadow magic seemed easier to use than the A'ras magic? What did that mean for her?

Alison waited and Carth recognized the way her brow crinkled. It was the same look she wore whenever the instructors tried demonstrating particularly difficult uses of magic.

"I was going to see if I could sense any more of the Hjan in the city," Carth answered.

"At night? Don't you think that's a little dangerous, especially with the rumors of the Reshian pushing into the city?"

Carth hadn't heard those rumors. They were nearly to the palace gate. If the token Invar had given her worked, she should be able to get out into the city, and from there... then she would be able to use her shadow magic. "I told you about my other ability," Carth said softly. She didn't want her voice to carry, and on a still night like tonight, she suspected it would.

"The one where you can hide?"

She nodded. It was more than that, but Alison didn't know that. "I think that's what gives me the ability to detect the Hjan."

Alison grabbed her wrist. "Does Invar know?"

"He knows. He thinks the same."

"Does he know you want to get back out into the city to search for them alone?"

Carth was thankful for the darkness that kept Alison from seeing her flush. "He knows I might return to the city."

Alison pulled on her arm. "You're doing this and Master Invar doesn't *know*?"

"Alison..."

Her friend shook her head. "Then I'm coming with you."

"You can't do that," Carth said. Not only didn't she want to get Alison in trouble, she didn't really want her friend to discover what she could do with shadows. "If I get caught, I can explain that I'm doing what I am for Invar."

"And I'm helping."

"Alison—"

"You're not going alone. If you try, I'll head up to the palace and tell him where you went."

"You wouldn't do that."

Alison cocked her head. "Try me, Carthenne Rel!"

Carth debated doing that, but couldn't risk Alison actually following through. And she'd do it because she thought she was protecting Carth, not trying to hurt her. Alison's willingness to risk their friendship for Carth's safety meant a lot. She could even claim that she intended to return to her room and sleep, and then sneak out later—but if she did that, she'd hurt Alison even more than she would by trying to push past her now.

"Fine. But you have to let me get past the gate."

Alison nodded.

They approached the gate and Carth saw a pair of A'ras standing on either side. Both held on to their magic—enough of it so that it burned softly within Carth's blood, leaving her skin tight. Neither pulled with much strength, but they didn't have to in order to react quickly.

Carth recognized only one of the A'ras, and her stomach flipped. It was an older man named Jeff who never cared for her when he taught, mostly because Carth took so long to use her magic. As Carth slowed, Alison pushed gently on her back, forcing her forward.

She stopped in front of the other A'ras, a woman slightly taller than Carth and with shadowed eyes that seemed to quickly dismiss both Carth and Alison.

"We need to enter the city," Carth said.

The A'ras glanced at her briefly. "You realize the time, ashai?"

Carth nodded, fishing the token from Invar from her pocket. "Master Invar asked me to—"

Jeff reached for the token and pressed a surge of magic through it. Carth held her breath, wondering if there was something to the token that would reveal when Invar had given it to her, or even something that might let them know that she was allowed into the city. Nothing happened.

"Invar may have given this to you, but if he did, it didn't trigger. Try again in the morning."

Carth started to argue, but Alison pulled her back, dragging her away from the wall.

"You argue with the A'ras stationed there and everyone is going to know that you attempted to come through," she said softly. As usual, Alison managed to have the reasonable response.

"I need to get back into the city," Carth said. She could wait until the morning, but if she did, she'd be going back out with Invar and wouldn't have the chance to see what she could do with the shadows.

Alison studied her for a moment. "What is it?"

Carth bit her lip. "Just a feeling I have," she said.

"A feeling. I think what you want to do is dangerous anyway—maybe it's best that you can't get out into the city tonight. Let's just… just go back to the cosak and get some sleep. Tomorrow you'll feel better and you can figure out what Master Invar wants you to do next."

Carth sighed. Arguing wouldn't do any good, and

besides that, Alison was right. She was tired and she would think better after getting some sleep. Only, she still didn't think she *could* sleep. She wanted answers that would only come on the other side of the wall.

Chapter 12

"Well, look who comes striding across the lawn," Alison said as they made their way toward the cosak.

Carth followed her gaze and saw Samis coming from the direction of the cosak, making his way straight toward them. "What do you think he wants?" Carth asked.

"Maybe to challenge me too?" Alison said.

Carth sucked in a breath. The challenge. She'd forgotten about it with everything that had happened with Invar. "How did it go?" she asked. Alison didn't seem injured, but with sparring, there were ways to mask injuries, so it was possible that she had been harmed but didn't show it.

Alison waved her hand. "Landon is stupid. He thinks he can hit me with brutality, but a few well-placed blows are all I needed to knock him out. Can't very well attack when you can't hold your sword."

At least Carth knew why Landon had seemed to be holding his arm when she'd seen him in the dining hall. "You *won?*"

"You don't have to sound so surprised," Alison said. "Like I said, he got arrogant. The others decided they didn't want to spar after it was done." A grin spread across her face. "A pretty good afternoon, if you ask me."

"Sorry I wasn't there."

"It sounds like Invar needed you. Besides, there will be plenty of other opportunities to watch me fighting."

She said the last quickly as Samis appeared, and Alison made no point of hiding her appraising gaze and swept it over him. Samis only laughed. "Good to see you too, Alison. Heard you gave Landon a broken wrist today."

Alison shrugged. "He'll heal fast enough."

"The A'ras he's paired with have already seen to that," Samis said.

"Maybe he won't think to spar with my friend the next time." She fixed Samis with a hard-eyed stare, which he met without turning away.

"I challenge her so we can both practice," Samis said. "Isn't that the point of the right to challenge?"

Alison shrugged. "I suppose. Is that why you're here tonight?"

Samis looked at Carth and shook his head. "Not why I'm here. Can I talk to Rel for a moment by myself?"

Alison looked at Carth and waited for her to nod. What would it matter if she spoke to Samis, especially as she wasn't going anywhere else tonight? "It's fine, Al."

Alison flashed a wide grin and tapped her wrist before leaving Carth standing with Samis. They stood silently for a few moments, Samis standing too close but Carth not wanting to be the one to take the first step away. Finally, she broke the silence.

"What do you want, Samis?"

"Always so direct, aren't you, Rel?"

"With you or with everyone?"

He laughed. "Both, I guess. I wanted to ask about what happened with Invar."

Carth sighed. "Why does everyone always keep coming to ask about him? Are you really that jealous of the fact that he's forcing me to study with him?"

Samis stared at her, eyes wide. "Forcing you? That's the way you see it?"

"What would you call it?" Carth asked. "He has me running through all the basic exercises, trying to get me faster."

"Because you need to get faster," Samis said.

"You think I don't know that? I realize how long it takes for me to do anything with my magic. I might not be that talented, but that doesn't mean I can't get better."

Samis was laughing at her.

Carth shot him as hard a look as she could. "What? Why are you laughing at me?"

"You might be slower to reach your magic, but once you have it, you're as talented as anyone, Rel."

"What are you trying to get from me?"

Samis shook his head, his laughter slowly dying off. "Why do I have to be trying to get anything from you? Can't I offer you a compliment?"

"No."

"Fine. What happened to your hand?" he asked.

Carth glanced briefly at the wrapped hand. It still throbbed, but with less intensity than before. She hoped that it wasn't as bad as it felt, and that by the morning she wouldn't have to wear the wrap around her hand; otherwise she'd have to tell Invar what had happened. He would know that she hadn't been injured during the attack.

"I burned it."

"How?"

"Fire."

He sniffed. "You know, you *could* provide a little more of an answer than that."

"Why do you care?"

Samis squeezed his eyes shut and forced a smile. "Fine. What were you doing out here by the gate at night?"

Carth glanced toward the gate. The shadowed forms of the two A'ras patrolling were visible from here. Invar had given her the token, but that hadn't mattered to them. And maybe the token hadn't been what she'd expected either. Maybe it only worked when he was with her.

"Rel?"

"I wanted to go back out into the city," she said.

He laughed, and in the otherwise silent night, the sound carried. "I thought you said you were attacked today. Why would you want to go back out and risk that happening again?"

How could she explain to him that she needed to return to the city? Not because of the Hjan—with the nausea she felt, she might be one of the few able to prepare before an attack came—but because she wanted to know what the shadows might be able to do for her.

"There was an attack, but I wanted to see if there was

anything else I can learn for Master Invar."

"Why do you think there's anything you can learn?"

Carth shook her head.

"Fine," Samis said with a shrug. "You don't have to share, and I won't share with you a way to get out into the city, then."

"There is no way to get into the city."

Samis flashed a smile. Carth hated that she flushed as he did. "You've been out into the city once. That means you've been given the way out."

"It doesn't work. I went to the gate—"

"It won't work at the gate, but there's another way it can."

"What are you playing at, Samis?"

He shrugged again. "Only that I'll help you get out into the city, but you'll have to tell me why you think you can find the attackers."

Carth glanced back toward the cosak. Alison would be there and expecting her to return, or at least for her to sleep off the fatigue from the day, but if Samis could show her how to get off the palace grounds and into the city, she wouldn't have to rely upon him in the future. What did it matter if she shared with him that she was shadow blessed?

"Fine. Once we get out into the city, I'll tell you."

Samis smiled again. Carth wanted to stab him for being so smug but decided that wouldn't help her get where she wanted. He started away from the gate, jogging across the lawn. She hurried after him, at first following silently, but the deeper he went onto the grounds, the more uncertain she was. Could he be leading her away for a reason?

She reached for her A'ras magic and almost gasped as her hand started throbbing. The magic pulsed in time with it, as if the power that burned within her rubbed against the pain in her hand. As she held on to that power, she realized Samis hadn't even reached for his connection yet.

"Where are you taking me?" she asked.

A few trees were nothing more than dark blurs as they ran. Samis pointed in the distance, beyond another stand of trees. "You wanted to get out into the city. So I'm taking you into the city."

The wall loomed up suddenly, a swath of darkness here where moonlight and light from the ashai buildings didn't reach. They were protected here, she realized, a place where no one would be able to know they were even here. Samis couldn't have picked a better place to try to cross the wall— or to harm her.

Carth held on to her magic, readying for whatever he might try. He motioned to the wall. "You should have been given something. The A'ras I'm with call it the Freedom Key. Not sure what Master Invar would have called it."

Carth clutched the token in her hand. "He didn't use anything quite so... dramatic."

Samis smiled. "I don't think they intended for me to learn that I could use the key to cross the wall, but I overheard them talking about how they used to sneak out into the city when they gained the rank of sai. I figure it's tradition that we do the same."

"The token didn't work at the gate," she said, pulling the

circular piece of stone from her pocket. It thrummed softly against her, more than it had when she hadn't held on to a trickle of the A'ras magic. She briefly tried to press magic into the stone, using it as a focus, much like she did with her knife, but nothing happened. Maybe that was why Jeff had thought the token not activated.

Samis pulled a long, slender stone from his pocket. As he did, magic flared in him. "I think you have to power through it as you use it. I don't know what happens at the gate, but out here…"

"Have you used this to cross the wall before?"

Samis glanced at the stone in his hand. "I've used it."

She detected the hesitation in him. "When?"

Samis looked to the wall before turning back to her. "Fine. I haven't crossed the wall before on my own, but I know it can be done. This was where Erik and Brody said they came. The wall can't have changed that much in the two years since they were raised."

Carth wondered. Invar said the Aras were placing layers of power into the wall, and that would change it, but then, the wall had also been breached by the Hjan, so maybe they countered each other. "What do you think we have to do?"

Samis held his stone out toward the wall, summoning magic through it. He grabbed at the ivy and started scaling the wall. When he reached the top of the wall, he swung his leg up… and bounced into the invisible barrier.

He landed on the ground with a grunt.

"Not like that, then?" she asked.

Sais shook his head. "Not like that. The key lets you

through somehow—we just have to figure out how it works."

"We? Why do you care about crossing the wall?"

Samis lay on the ground with his eyes closed. "You want to get over there, and so do I. Like I said, if we work together, we'll be more likely to succeed."

Carth thought about kicking him. "Why do you want to get to the other side?"

Samis flushed. She'd never seen him flustered in all the time he'd been here. In some ways, it was actually endearing. "You don't know what it's like to be someplace so long you don't know what else is out there."

Carth laughed bitterly. "I think I do."

Samis sat up, rubbing his back and grimacing. How badly was he injured? She didn't want to have to carry him back to the cosak and explain what had happened. With Samis, she wasn't even sure she *could* carry him. He was much larger than Invar, more muscular, and she doubted she would get very far before he fell on top of her... now, why did that thought make her flush again?

"No, Rel. You know what it's like to be here for the last few years, but that's nothing. You have memories of a time before you came here. All of my memories are of this place, of learning how to reach for magic, and of wandering these grounds."

The frustration she'd felt toward Samis faded. "You don't have any memories of a time before you came here?"

He shrugged. "Maybe some, but none of them is clear. Even my memories of my parents are faint, faded."

"When did you last seen them?"

It was his turn to offer a bitter laugh. "When they brought me here."

Carth blinked. At least she'd had the chance to know her parents until she was twelve. She had memories of them—mostly *good* memories—and also memories of what it was like outside the palace walls.

"Maybe you need to get beyond the wall more than I do," she said.

"I don't know about *more than*. I'll take the same amount."

Carth pulled on her magic, drawing it through her blood, almost screaming as it throbbed against her injured hand, and sent it into the stone. She was tired. All the effort she'd exerted through the day had exhausted her, and she wouldn't have even tried to reach for it if there hadn't been the hope of reaching the other side. Holding on to the stone, she scrambled up the vine and tried kicking her foot over.

Like Samis, she struck an invisible barrier and bounced back.

Carth had the wherewithal to twist around as she fell so that she landed mostly on her feet, crouching next to Samis.

"You don't have to show off with falling, too," he said.

"I'm not showing off."

"You're not lying here next to me with your backside throbbing, either."

Carth laughed and caught herself before anyone heard them. "I don't think this is going to work. Maybe the masters realized the ashai were sneaking off the grounds and prepared a way to hold them inside. Either way, I don't think we're getting out with our keys, not without having someone with more potential let us free."

"I don't think potential is the issue. This is more an issue of… strength. It's like whatever is in place here is too strong for us."

"Maybe it is here," she said.

"What?"

"Come on," she told him, "unless your sensitive backside hurts too much to follow me."

Samis got up carefully, rubbing his back as he did. "I don't know what hurts worse, my back or my pride at having you see me fall like that."

Carth smiled. "Hopefully only your back. Your pride doesn't have to worry about what I might think."

She moved along the wall, keeping close to the ivy and staying within the shadows of the wall. At this time of night, it was easy enough to do. She tried reaching for the shadows and wrapping them around her, but though the connection was there, it was too faint for her to do anything with. That she detected it at all gave her hope that she'd be able to find a way to cross.

They stopped at the section of the wall damaged by the Hjan. Masons had repaired it, and the A'ras masters had started placing barriers within it, but she hoped there might be some residual weakness remaining that would let the two of them cross.

"Are you sure this is a good idea, Rel?" Samis asked.

"Not at all."

She pressed power through the stone and started up the ivy near the damaged section of the wall. Reaching the top, she pushed even more strength through the stone and kicked her foot at the same time.

Momentum carried her up and over the wall, where she disappeared into the darkness of the other side.

She waited, and within a moment, Samis followed, landing next to her with more grace than he had with his fall.

"Well?" he said.

"Well, what?"

"Now you have to tell me your secret."

Chapter 13

Samis let Carth lead the way through the street. As soon as she had landed on this side of the wall, a sense of the shadows had surged through her. She almost wrapped herself within them and created a cloak, but decided against it. Samis might want answers, but she wouldn't give him more questions as well.

The city felt different at night than during the day. She thought that had to do with more than her sense of the shadows, but maybe that was all it was. There was a pulsing sort of vibrancy to the city, one that she felt through her bones. Music and song drifted along the street, mixing with that sense of vibrancy, or perhaps causing it. A few crowds of people moved along the street, but mostly they came in pairs or threes.

Since coming to Nyaesh, Carth had felt comfortable at night. Now that she knew she was shadow blessed, she understood the reason. There was nothing about the shadows that frightened her, not even when she was a child.

"Where are we going?" Samis asked.

Without intending to, Carth led them away from the palace and toward the docks. "Wandering," she told him.

"Looks like you have someplace you're leading us."

Carth grunted but didn't answer. She glanced at Samis and realized that he'd taken off his A'ras sash. He didn't even carry his sword. "Don't you feel underprepared?"

"Don't you?"

She slipped her knife from the sheath with a quick flourish before shoving it back. "No."

"Good thing you're with me, then. Besides, I've never had any issues on patrol. It's mostly a show of force so we keep the Reshian from the city."

"Not when it comes to the Hjan."

"We're not going to run into them tonight, are we?"

Carth thought about the nausea she'd felt when she'd detected the Hjan before. "I hope not."

"Good. I haven't even had a chance to practice with the Reshian yet. I'm not sure I'm ready for these Hjan."

They turned down Doland Street, the long road that ran toward the docks. Carth paused, watching people as they moved past her. In the daylight, when she'd been with Invar, the crowds had parted around them, giving Invar space. Perhaps her as well. At night, and without her sash, the people paid her no more mind than anyone else making their way through the streets. There was a strange reassurance in that anonymity. Maybe the Hjan wouldn't even know she was here.

"There's so many people still out." A sense of wonder filled Samis's voice, and Carth smiled.

"It never really slows down."

"The city?"

Carth shrugged. "We're along the Maladon River. Lots of cargo comes through here, moving toward the sea. People come from all over, and many have never been to a city this size. They only want to stay out." That had been part of the reason she'd always had success collecting scraps. Not the time of day—though that had something to do with it; the more men drank, the easier it became for her to slip a purse free from a pocket.

"Was it always like this when you lived here?" Samis asked.

"I never lived in this part of the city. After my parents died, I stayed along the docks. One of the innkeepers took me in and gave me a place to stay, food to eat." And she hadn't asked anything other than that Carth help sell baked goods for her. Even at that, Carth hadn't done a very good job. She'd been much more interested in stealing, and wandering the city; anything other than the simple task Vera had asked of her.

"I didn't know your parents died."

Carth glanced at him. "What did you think happened?"

He shrugged. "Same as with the rest of us, I guess. Parents realize there's potential they can't reach and they bring you to the palace. Most of us. Quite a few are born in the palace, so there's really nowhere else to go, like Landon."

Carth smiled. "I don't know what my parents knew about my potential, only that they brought me to Nyaesh, and I suspect they wanted me to study with the A'ras."

"You didn't know?"

They were farther down the street, and now the sound of the water rushing along the shore parted the silence of the night. Voices along the street were more muted, and the shadows came more frequently. An alley led off the street and Carth almost turned down it, thinking of the herbalist who had once been so welcoming.

"I don't know what they intended for me," she said. "They never told me."

"You're not from Nyaesh."

"I think everyone is well aware of that, thank you very much," she said.

Samis glanced at her and shook his head. "That's not what I mean. Why did you think you were coming to the city if not to study with the A'ras?"

"This wasn't the first city we stopped in," Carth said. She thought of the line of villages and towns her parents had brought her through before they'd reached Nyaesh. They had stayed in each of them for varying lengths. Some, like Tripol, they were in for nearly a year. Others, like the village Sahar, they stayed for only a few weeks. Carth had memories of most, though she didn't know why her parents had continued to move.

"You're an interesting person, Carthenne Rel."

Carth rounded on him, slipping her knife from the sheath without thinking. "How do you know my full name?"

Samis flushed and took a step back from her. "I—"

She jabbed the knife at him and his eyes went wide. It took her a moment to realize *why*.

Shadows swirled around the end of the knife. She had reached for the shadows without intending to and had nearly attacked Samis with them. Recognizing that, she released the connection to the shadows, flushing slightly.

"How did you know my name?" she asked again.

"I've overheard you and Alison talking. The two of you carry on sometimes and talk louder than you realize. I don't know why you don't use your full name. It's nice."

She shook her head and slipped the knife back into her sheath. "Only my mother called me Carthenne."

"You let Alison call you that."

"I don't think I could stop Alison if I wanted to," she said.

Samis grinned. "She can be a little strong-willed, can't she?"

That might have been one of the nicest things anyone had ever called Alison. "That's why she's such a great friend."

They continued along the street and Carth made no secret of the fact that she headed straight toward the docks. Samis said nothing until they reached River Road. "What was that?" he asked.

"It was nothing."

He shook his head, his gaze drifting to the knife sheathed at her waist. "It was something, Rel. I've never seen anything like it. I know you're strong when you pull on your potential, so I'm not sure what that might be." He pulled his gaze up to her eyes. "Is that the secret you don't want me to know about?"

She licked her lips. It was bad enough that Alison and now

Master Invar knew of her ability with shadows, but Samis too? How many more would learn that she was shadow blessed?

"You know that I'm not from Nyaesh. My parents are from a place called Ih-lash. Some of the people are born with a connection to shadows that allows them to hide. They're called shadow blessed."

"And you?"

She met his eyes. "I think I'm one of the shadow blessed."

"Think? You don't know? You can do... whatever that was and you don't know?"

Carth took a deep breath. "Invar thinks that's the reason I'm able to detect the Hjan. He thinks there's something about being one of the shadow blessed that lets me know when they're near."

Samis watched her for a while. Carth wondered what was going on behind the deep blue eyes. Would he think she didn't belong studying with the A'ras?

"Is that why you're always a step slow?" he finally asked.

"What's that supposed to mean?"

"When you reach for your potential. You're always a step slow. Does it have anything to do with this other ability of yours?"

"I don't know. When we're on the other side of the wall, I'm not able to use it. The power placed into the wall by the A'ras masters keeps me from it. It's only when we're on this side of the wall that I can sense it again."

"That's why you wanted to come out here tonight, isn't it?" When she didn't answer, he frowned. "What else can you do with it?"

"What do you mean?"

He shrugged. "You said you could use the shadows to hide?"

Carth took a step back from him and pulled on the shadows, creating a cloak. As soon as she did, the sounds became more muted and yet somehow sharper. Samis gasped.

"Where did you go?"

She released the cloak. It had been so long since she had used her ability, long enough that she wasn't sure it would still work for her the way it should. Finding that she could still use the shadows as easily as she once had reassured her.

"That's what I can do."

Samis blinked. "How? I mean… how?"

"I don't know. It's not something I can even explain. The man who told me about the shadow blessed didn't know anything about it either, but told me that it wasn't uncommon in Ih-lash. I think my parents knew what I could do."

"Think? You don't know?"

"They never said anything about it before…"

"Then how did you know?"

"My father used to play games with me. My mother, too. I think the games were meant to draw out any ability I might have with the shadows."

"I bet you could use the shadows in other ways. Look at the way you sent it through the knife! And if there are people like you in the world who can detect the Hjan, I wonder why the masters don't try to get their help."

Carth hadn't asked that question before and realized that

she should have. Why *hadn't* the masters gone looking for others from Ih-lash? That was a question she'd have to ask the next time she worked with Invar.

"How did you learn to use them?" he asked. "The shadows. You said your parents never taught you, but who did if not them?"

"There was a man... he found me in the city, or maybe I found him. I thought he might have had something to do with what happened to them, but he showed me what it meant for me to be shadow blessed."

She moved away from Samis and made her way toward the Wounded Lyre. She had come this way without fully knowing where she was going, but she wasn't surprised that she had found her way here.

The tavern looked no different than it had five years ago. Maybe more faded, the painted sign hanging from the entrance a lighter shade than it had once been, but lights still burned brightly within and the sound of music drifted out, a vibrant sound, and one that reminded her of simpler times.

But had they been so simple?

She hadn't known much about her shadow abilities, but those had been some of the hardest days for her, especially in the months immediately following losing her parents. Kel and Etan hadn't been particularly welcoming, though Kel had eventually become someone she cared about—and another person she had lost.

Maybe she romanticized that time, or maybe it was that the tavern had been the last home she'd had before going with the A'ras.

"This was the place, wasn't it?" Samis asked.

"This was it," she agreed.

"Do you want to go in?"

Carth shook her head. "What would I say? Even if they remembered me, what would I say?"

"Wouldn't they be happy to see you?"

"I... I don't know. I left without saying anything to them. I didn't want goodbyes, and I didn't want it to be harder than it needed to be."

"That seems like it would be worse."

"Children go missing all the time in this part of the city," she said quickly, remembering the words Vera had once said to her. They had been a warning, not a threat, and one that had, in a way, hardened something inside of Carth. Hopefully fewer children went missing now, after what she'd done, but she hadn't remained around long enough to know.

"You don't think they would worry?"

"They would have worried more about having me go with the A'ras. Not all see them the way you do. Some fear them."

"Us. Not them."

Carth nodded. "Fine. Us."

Him saying it didn't make it true for her. As much as she might try to be a part of the A'ras, she still felt like she was apart from them, different enough because of her inability to reach her magic as easily as others, or because of the fact that she was older than most of the ashai, or now even because she'd been chosen to work with Invar, something

133

most thought some sort of honor but Carth knew to be remedial lessons.

"Where do you want to go now?" Samis asked.

The door opened to the Wounded Lyre, letting out more of the music and a flutter of warmth. The unmistakable scent of Vera's cooking came with it and she sighed. "Back to the palace," she said.

Samis glanced over but didn't say a word.

Chapter 14

The next few days passed slowly, almost painfully. Invar didn't come for her again, and did not summon her, either. She had gone to the palace the first morning after she and Samis had snuck into the city and had been turned away. Master Invar was not prepared for his student. That was all she was told. The next day was the same. And the following day, she was told he would find her when he was ready to resume her lessons.

In some ways, not working with Invar was worse than when she had been allowed to study with him. At least then she hadn't had to see the pitying looks of the other students at the fact that she had returned to the ashai classes. Carth kept to herself, sitting near the back of the class, letting her mind drift.

Her hand healed more quickly than she would have imagined. The day after the burn, the skin had peeled away, almost as if she had been in the sun for too long, leaving it red and sensitive, but not raw and blistered like it had been the day before. Carth had kept it wrapped that day mostly to protect it, but by the second day, she was able to leave it uncovered.

Had it healed so quickly because she'd been using A'ras magic? The A'ras generally healed from injuries rapidly, something she knew came from the connection to the magic, but she had never experienced a real injury to know. By the fourth day after the burn, there was no way to know that she'd been injured, other than the throbbing beneath the surface of her hand that never completely went away.

Alison sat next to her, almost dutifully. Carth sensed a hint of resentment from her friend when she shared how she had snuck out of the palace grounds with Samis, but Alison never said anything to suggest she was jealous, only acting slightly colder than usual.

And Samis continued his patrols. He would join the ashai every evening, but he was gone through the day and would eat quickly before disappearing once more. It was such a difference now that he had been raised to sai. Landon as well, but he had practically stopped coming to the dining hall, making his infrequent appearances that much more noticeable.

By the time the summons to meet with Invar came, Carth had begun to think he no longer wanted to work with her.

It happened nearly a week after she and Samis had snuck off the grounds. A younger woman came to her, an A'ras named Racha who had only recently been raised, and slipped a folded piece of paper to her. Inside were instructions to meet Invar.

Carth's stomach sank when she realized where he wanted

to meet. It was the same place where she and Samis had crossed the wall.

Racha nodded and disappeared, leaving Carth staring at the page silently.

"What is it?" Alison whispered.

"Only Invar wanting to meet."

"I thought that was a good thing."

"Not *where* he wants to meet."

Alison's eyes widened as she seemed to understand.

The rest of the class went by painfully slowly, and when it finished, Carth was tired, irritable from her slow access to her magic, and leery about what Invar intended by having her meet him there.

Carth made her way toward the wall with a nervous flutter in her stomach. It was nothing like the flutter she'd had when the Hjan had attacked, but that didn't make her feel any better.

He was already waiting. The master wore a plain gray robe tied around the waist with a thick sash of maroon. In some ways, it made him more stately.

Another man waited with Invar. He had black hair the color of a moonless night and eyes that were nearly as black. A shirt of shimmering fabric that matched his eyes hung loose about him. There was no sash, nothing that marked him as A'ras.

What, then?

When she approached, Invar turned to her, a broad smile spreading across his face. "Ms. Rel," he said.

Carth glanced at the other man, but he remained near

the wall, staying near the ivy and in the traces of shadows found during a bright day like today.

"Master Invar."

Carth hoped he would tell her why he hadn't been willing to meet with her and why it had taken nearly a week for him to get back to her. "I thought we should return to the location of the first attack and see what else you might be able to tell me from that day," he started, as if no time had passed since the last time they were together.

Carth glanced from Invar to the other man. Was Invar going to introduce him, or did he intend to keep her questioning why he had brought another here? "I've told you all I can about that day," she said.

"You've said what you saw, but you haven't shared what you *felt*."

Her heart fluttered. "Scared."

"I suspect you were, Ms. Rel. A natural feeling for one to have when faced with the Hjan, but that is not exactly the sensation I am asking about."

"What do you want to know?"

"You are of Ih-lash, and you claim that you felt nausea when we were attacked."

Carth glanced from Invar to the man behind him. The comment seemed directed at him, rather than toward her, but why would Invar make a comment like that?

"That's what happened."

"Then again a week ago, when we were in the city, you felt the same nausea. You used your shadow blessing to protect us." The slight edge in his voice made it seem like

Invar didn't completely believe that, though Carth didn't blame him. She still wasn't entirely certain what she'd done, but the shadows had been involved.

"I did."

"That is not how the shadow blessing works," the man said. He had a strange clipped accent to his voice, almost a singsong way of speaking, one that in some respects reminded her of... her father.

"You're from Ih-lash," she said.

The man took a step toward her and she noticed the way the shadows trailed after him.

Not only from Ih-lash, but shadow blessed as well.

Carth tried reaching for the shadows, but failed.

The wall—the A'ras magic layered upon the wall—still prevented her. Why didn't it prevent him?

"I made that claim, once," he said. He tipped his head, eyeing Carth appraisingly. "You do not look like one of the Ih-lash." His gaze went to her hair, then her face. "Your hair is too brown, and your eyes are much too light."

Carth touched her hair, running her hand across it. The chestnut brown had always been more like her mother's hair than her father's, but she had often claimed she had his eyes. In some ways, her father had features that matched this man, with similar coloring.

"I..."

"I came as we agreed, Invar. There is nothing I can offer. She is not what you think."

Invar watched Carth, his face clouding. Was it disappointment that he wore?

139

"Jicanl, I can only tell you what—"

The Ih-lash man started up the wall, climbing the ivy quickly. At the top, the shadows seemed to coalesce around him and he kicked over.

Carth almost gasped.

Invar turned to her, but she ignored him.

This man was shadow blessed. When he'd stood near her, with the shadows trailing around him, she had suspected but hadn't known for sure. Now... there was no way to do what he did without having that ability.

Carth grabbed the token Invar had given her—she still carried it with her, even if she hadn't left the city in days—and started pressing A'ras magic through it as she climbed the ivy.

"Ms. Rel!"

She ignored him, and when she reached the top of the wall, she pressed through the token, swinging her leg.

But met resistance.

Carth grunted in frustration, clinging so that she didn't fall, but started to slip. She had strength for one more attempt and kicked her leg up again. This time when she did, she scrambled for the connection to the shadows. The sense came slowly, and she pulled on it, holding on to it with a ferocity. The man on the other side of the wall would be able to show her about her abilities! She needed to reach him.

Her foot eased through the barrier, and then she was falling.

Carth twisted, drawing on the A'ras magic to help her as she landed.

The man was nowhere on this side of the wall.

She reached for the shadows. If he *was* here, he would have a connection to the shadows, and she might be able to determine what it was. Free from the A'ras suppression, her connection to the shadows surged.

Almost immediately, she detected the slight difference in the shadows. Carth traced the connection, noting how it made its way along the street and away from the docks.

She ran.

Holding on to the cloak of shadows seemed to make her gait swift. She refused to let him get too far ahead of her. He would have answers for her—answers that she suspected Invar intended for her to have—but first she had to catch him.

As she ran, she realized she wasn't fast enough. Through the connection to the shadow magic, she noted that he continued to pull away from her, gradually growing more and more distant.

Carth pulled on the A'ras magic and mixed it with the connection to the shadows.

She ran, racing through the streets. If she caught him, would he be able to share with her what it meant for her to be shadow blessed? Would she learn how he managed to use the shadows on the other side of the wall, even though the A'ras magic worked through them?

Near the edge of the city, a massive wall rose up, ringing the entirety of the city until it reached the docks. Right there, the sense of the shadows changed.

Carth paused, focusing on her connection to the

shadows, trying to determine if she still even detected the other shadow blessed.

She walked along the wall, holding her shadow cloak as she went. She detected something here but wasn't sure what it was. It didn't feel the same as the shadows. She frowned. If she didn't find him, would Invar help? He'd managed to bring him to the palace in the first place, likely to determine if she really was shadow blessed. Invar hadn't believed her, but then, Carth had never lived in Ih-lash and didn't know that she didn't look like the shadow blessed.

After making her way along the wall, she still hadn't discovered anything that made her believe Jicanl remained in the city. With a sigh, she started back toward the palace.

As she did, a wave of nausea rolled through her.

Carth froze.

It could be a coincidence, or it could be the Hjan.

She'd used the shadow magic more than she had in years, and maybe that had unsettled her.

The sense came again.

This time, she knew it came from her sense of the Hjan.

Worse, the sense came from near the palace.

Chapter 15

As Carth ran toward the palace, she wondered what she was doing. If the Hjan attacked, did she really think there was anything she could do? The masters were there, and they would keep the palace and the grounds safe, something Carth wouldn't be able to help with. She'd gotten lucky the last time she faced the Hjan, and the time before that, she'd only survived because Invar and the other masters had appeared.

The nausea intensified.

This was worse than the last attack.

Holding on to the connection to the shadows eased the nausea somewhat, at least keeping her from vomiting all over herself. She maintained the shadow cloak and held tightly to the connection to the A'ras magic as well.

The palace wall loomed into view.

An explosion thundered.

Carth felt the force of it nearly throw her back. Had she not already been holding both the shadow blessing and the A'ras magic, she might have fallen, but instead, she jumped.

And sailed through the air, landing nearly a dozen steps from where she had been.

Carth almost stumbled as she landed. Had she used A'ras magic to leap? There were those of the A'ras who *could* use their magic in such a way, but Carth had never managed to do anything quite like that before. Or was it the shadow blessing? She thought of how she had once used the shadows, wrapping herself in them as she swam through the dark, trying to help Kel.

She leaped again, and again she sailed.

Carth laughed, jumping again and again. Each jump took her the same distance.

Another explosion thundered from the palace wall.

Carth launched herself toward it.

A section of the wall had crumbled. As she arrived, she saw a line of A'ras facing five hooded figures. The had to be Hjan by the way they flickered as they moved, having a strange way they managed to attack, and as they did, the nausea rolled through her.

Invar and Lyanna faced against one of the Hjan, pushing him back. The other four fought among the A'ras, moving with a blinding speed as they flickered and then disappeared.

Carth unsheathed her knife and pressed A'ras magic through it. As she did, she added the shadow magic as well. She leaped forward, still wrapped in shadows.

She struck one of the Hjan, and he fell.

Carth jumped back, trying to get clear, but on this side of the wall, her jumps didn't carry quite as far.

Two of the Hjan turned toward her, though neither was

the man she'd protected Invar from.

Carth pulled on the shadows and had to do so at the expense of losing the connection to the A'ras magic. She wrapped them around her, cloaking herself, praying that she remained hidden enough that they wouldn't—or couldn't—see her.

Without the damage to the wall, she doubted she would have managed. She pressed on the shadows that she cloaked herself with and sent them surging through the knife.

She sliced at one of the Hjan.

Her knife caught the man on the arm and he fell. Blackness coursed through him.

The other Hjan swept brightly glowing knives toward her and she jumped back, trying to hold on to the shadows as she did. The man reached his fallen soldier and, with a quick flicker, they both disappeared.

She glanced around. The first Hjan she'd hit was missing, and the two facing the masters pressed them back. Carth surged through her knife and stabbed at the nearest.

It struck the Hjan in the back.

With a gasp, he started to fall.

The other Hjan flickered to him, grabbed him, and then disappeared.

Carth almost released her connection to the shadows, but decided against it. When she looked around, the attack appeared over. Invar scanned the yard, his gaze narrowed. He suspected her.

She raced through the yard, away from the fractured wall, away from the fallen Hjan, and reached the cosak. As she ran, the shadows slowly trailed away from her until she wasn't able to hold them with the same strength, eventually losing them altogether.

Samis stood at the door to the cosak. When the shadows completely disappeared, he frowned. "Where have you been?"

"Here," she said.

"There was another attack, but you knew that, didn't you?"

"I heard it."

"You were there again."

"I…" She didn't want to lie to Samis about this. "Just let me in and I'll tell you whatever you want."

Samis glanced past her and then pushed open the cosak door. Carth hurried past and reached her room, where she fell onto her bed.

As she lay there, the loud sounds of voices echoed from the other side of the wall. It was the sound of chaos and the remnants of battle. Carth wanted nothing more than to lie where she was, pull the shadows around her, and sleep, but she couldn't. Her mind raced, working through what she had seen, how the man from Ih-lash had raced from the palace, and the timing of the attack. Had she been within the palace walls, there wouldn't have been anything she could have done. Thankfully, she had been outside the walls, and she had been able to use the shadows. Had she not, she didn't know if she would have managed to help stop the Hjan.

A pounding on her door startled her.

Carth reached for A'ras magic, which came slowly, pulled like thick syrup from her. She focused it on the knife, letting the sense of the magic flow through her and into the knife. She wouldn't be unprepared for whoever was on the other side of the door. Had she the ability to reach the shadows, she'd simply have wrapped herself in them, letting them cloak her completely.

"Rel!" she heard through the door. "I know you're in there!"

Samis.

She owed him for letting her back into the cosak. He could have turned her away and left her outside, where she'd have to answer other questions, but he hadn't. And as far as she knew, he hadn't shared with anyone what he'd learned the night they'd snuck away from the palace.

She pulled the door open a crack and peered outside. "What do you want?"

Samis glanced down the hall before pushing his face into the crack. He was stronger than her and could've tried pushing his way into the room, but he didn't. "That's all you're going to say to me? What is going on, Rel?"

"There was another attack."

"I gathered that from the way the masters had Landon and me stand watch over the cosak. I've never been asked to do anything more than observe, and now they're giving us assignments?"

"The rest of the A'ras were needed," Carth said.

"The rest? As in, *all* of the A'ras remaining in the palace?"

"That's what the rest means, Samis."

He leaned on the door and let out a long breath. Carth stepped away and he fell forward.

"What happened?" he asked.

She shook her head. "I don't know. There were five Hjan attacking."

"Five? And the last time when there were three, it took all of the masters working together to push him back."

"Yes."

"So what happened?"

Carth turned away, releasing some of the hold she had on the A'ras magic. She didn't need it here, not with Samis. Besides, it increased the throbbing in her hand the longer she held the connection.

"Rel?"

When she still didn't answer, he positioned himself in front of her. "What happened, Carth?"

She took a breath. She *wanted* to tell him what happened, but she hated the idea of sharing too much with him, risking more of the strange glances she got so often as it was. Coming from Samis, they would be that much worse.

"I used the shadows," she said softly.

Samis frowned. "I didn't think you could use them on this side of the wall. I thought the layering placed by the masters prevented you."

"It does. Invar... Invar called me to meet with him. There was a man with him. From Ih-lash."

"Your homeland."

She nodded. "I... he claimed I wasn't of Ih-lash. I think that was what Invar wanted to know. He wanted to know whether I was telling him the truth."

"I've seen what you can do with the shadows!"

Carth looked down at her hands. Invar had seen it too, she thought. Maybe more than she wanted, now that she'd used them against the Hjan attack. "I don't know what he's seen. I don't think he knows either."

"I don't understand why that had you so shook up."

She looked up to him, a pleading look in her eyes. "He used the shadows, Samis. On *this* side of the wall. When I realized that was what he did, I chased him."

"You *chased* him?"

She bit her lip, her hand drifting to the knife. She still held on to the slight hum of the magic as it coursed through her, and her hand throbbed with it. "I climbed the wall after him and chased him through the city."

"And Master Invar saw this?"

"I'm sorry, Samis. He knows how we got out now. I tried catching the man from Ih-lash, but he disappeared."

"Well, I supposed he used the shadows the same as you."

"Better," she said. That was the reason she had really wanted to catch him. If she could learn how to use the shadows in the same way, how much better would that make her abilities? "I lost him. As I was making my way back to the palace, I saw the explosion. I got to the wall and saw the Hjan and I just…"

Samis chuckled, shaking his head. "You attacked, didn't you? You used the shadows as you attacked."

Carth nodded. "I did what I had to in order to help the A'ras. I think I cut one Hjan—maybe another—and then they left."

"They left?"

Carth took a breath. "I think the shadows did something to them. I don't understand how."

"When you said you used the shadows to cover yourself, I knew it was more than that. I saw the way you pushed it through the knife, Rel. Maybe it's the way your shadow blessing works with the A'ras magic. Whatever it is, if it keeps them from returning..."

"That's just it. I don't think it keeps them from returning. The one I got when Invar was attacked used some sort of light to clear it from him and then he disappeared."

"This wasn't the first time you did it."

She shook her head.

"What about then? Was that the first time?"

"The man who attacked my parents... I... I used something similar with him, but I didn't know what it was then any more than I do now."

"Did he get away?"

"The shadows killed him."

Samis stared at her. "Who was with you that night?"

"Avera. A man named Jhon. He was the one who taught me what I could do."

Samis rubbed at his chin. "I think you need to talk to Master Avera, Rel. You need to understand what's going on and if there's some way you can use this ability to help the A'ras. Listen, you've already shown that you can tell when an attack is coming, that you can feel it. You need to see if there's anything else you can do that can help. Like maybe working with the A'ras so that they can find a way to keep these attacks from coming."

Carth knew she should. What Samis said made sense, but admitting her ability with the shadows was hard, especially when she didn't even know what it was she could do. If she could have reached Jicanl, she might have found a way to get answers, but there weren't any.

"I don't know what I should do," she said softly.

"I think you should find Master Avera. Or Master Invar. If there's anything you can do to help with this…"

"The boy is correct, Ms. Rel."

She turned, her stomach sinking.

Chapter 16

Master Invar stood in her doorway, a massive gash on one harm and blood staining his forehead. His hand rested on his sword, and a steady burning throbbing radiated from him as he held on to his magic. How had she missed it before now?

"Master Invar," Samis said.

Invar frowned at him. "Mr. Gold. I would have a word with Ms. Rel."

Samis offered Carth an apologetic look and then hurried from the room. Master Invar closed the door after him, pausing briefly as he pushed it closed, resting his hand on the frame. It took Carth a moment to realize that he sealed her in.

When he turned back to her, his face was an unreadable cloud. "Tell me, Ms. Rel, what happened back there?"

Her throat was dry and she licked her lips. How much did she tell him? How much did he already know?

If he discovered her keeping anything from him, she suspected she knew how he would react. Not well.

"The Hjan attacked."

Invar smiled briefly. "Yes. I am aware that the Hjan attacked. What I am interested in is what happened before the Hjan attacked."

"You mean with Jicanl?"

"Yes."

"You brought him to find out if I'm really shadow blessed."

"I thought it would be prudent to learn. I can assure you, it was most difficult to reach one of the shadow blessed not affiliated with..." He shook his head. "Regardless, know that it was especially difficult to convince him to come here. There are not many who remain."

"What do you mean? You could go to Ih-lash and find someone. Jhon told me that—"

His face darkened briefly at the mention of Jhon. "You don't know?" he asked the question mostly to himself. Invar turned to the window and stared out it, his back to Carth. "How long has it been since you were in Ih-lash?"

She shook her head. "I don't know. My parents are of Ih-lash, and I think I was born there, but I don't have any memories of it."

Invar turned to her. "I don't think your parents were from Ih-lash."

Carth shook her head. They had always told her about Ih-lash, sharing with her what they had left, though never why. They had wandered from city to village, never settling for long. When they reached Nyaesh, Carth had expected to move on from here, but this had been the place she'd stayed the longest.

153

"My father—"

Invar nodded. "It is possible that your father was of Ih-lash. You have eyes that almost could be of old Ih. That was why I believed you even if Jicanl does not. Your hair and your complexion, though, are not those of one from Ih-lash."

"What are you saying?"

Invar shrugged. "I'm saying that I don't think your mother is of Ih-lash. It would explain how you can reach the A'ras magic. I suspect that she could, and knew that she could, which was why she brought you here."

Carth didn't know what to say. Her parents had always told her so much about Ih-lash. They had spoken of it in such warm ways, with a fondness that made Carth wish they'd never left. Maybe if they hadn't, she would have learned of her ability with the shadows sooner. If they had never left, she might not have lost her parents.

So many ifs.

"My parents told me about Ih-lash. That was their home, even if it was never mine."

"Ah, Ms. Rel." He tried to sound reassuring but failed.

"What aren't you telling me, Invar?" She shouldn't be so curt with him, or so demanding, but she needed to know.

"Ih-lash is no more, Ms. Rel."

"No more?"

"It hasn't been for many years. You couldn't have been born there. The people of that land… they are all scattered. That's why finding Jicanl was so difficult. The shadow blessed hide in… well, in the shadows."

"I don't understand."

"You don't have to understand, Ms. Rel. Your father might have been of Ih-lash, and if what you tell me is true and you can reach the shadows, then it is likely that he, at least, was from Ih-lash. Your mother... she would have been from somewhere else."

Carth turned away from him, her mind racing. Hadn't her parents both told her about Ih-lash? Or *had* it been only her father? The books she'd rescued from her home were written in old Ih, a language Carth had barely begun to learn. She thought her mother had prized them, but what if it had been the opposite? What if it had been her father?

"Why wouldn't they have told me?" she whispered.

"For your safety."

"I don't understand."

Invar moved in front of her and waited until she looked up at him, meeting his eyes. "Ih-lash was destroyed because of the shadow blessed. They were—are—hunted."

"Why?"

"I didn't know that at first, but I'm beginning to understand."

"Why?"

"Because they are feared. Because you can use the shadows in ways others do not understand. Because you are what they are not."

"Who? Who did this to Ih-lash?"

"The answer to that is complicated, and I'm afraid I would be unable to do it justice. For now, know that it is tied to an ancient argument."

The Hjan. Carth didn't need for him to say it to know in

her heart that it was true. It explained why her parents would have been killed, why they had been hunted, destroyed by Felyn. It explained why Felyn had remained in Nyaesh, especially if he thought there was a chance that she might be shadow blessed as well. In that way, she was lucky to live.

"What does this mean for me?" she whispered.

"Mean?"

"Will you kick me out of the A'ras?"

Invar smiled slightly. "Ms. Rel, you may be shadow blessed, but you can reach the flame as well. It burns within you. That is why you are protected behind these walls." His gaze drifted to the window. "Mostly protected. You are A'ras as well. You do not have to be of Nyaesh to be A'ras, though I wonder if your mother does not share common ancestors. A shame that we will never be able to ask."

Carth touched the necklace she wore, the one with her mother's ring on it. She'd never been able to bring herself to actually wear it on her finger, so she kept it on a chain as a reminder instead.

Invar nodded, as if he had decided something. "Was that your help with the Hjan?"

Carth nodded numbly. She wasn't sure what to make of what Invar had told her. So much of what she'd thought she knew was wrong. Her parents had hidden secrets from her—maybe for her safety, but that didn't change the fact that they had kept things from her.

"The same help you offered me?" he asked.

She nodded.

"Interesting. Jicanl didn't think the shadows could be

used in such a way. How was it that you managed?"

Carth looked down at the knife. Each time she'd used the shadows in that way, she'd been using the knife as a focus. "It was this," she said, unsheathing her knife.

Within the A'ras, it was common for the ashai to possess knives. Many brought them with them. The expectation was that, when raised to full A'ras, she would craft her own. The one she possessed had come from a fallen A'ras, a man she had once thought had killed her mother.

Invar held his hand out for the knife, and Carth reluctantly let him take it.

"Where did you acquire this?"

"When my mother died, there were three A'ras who also died."

Invar closed his eyes. "I knew them."

"I'm sorry."

"You have nothing to be sorry about, Ms. Rel. Their death was at the hands of the Hjan, not the result of anything that you did."

"I took this knife from one of them."

Invar frowned. Magic surged through the knife briefly before fading again. "That is unlikely."

"It's true. Al-shad"—she still remembered his name after all this time—"had it on him."

Invar flipped the knife around and handed it back to her. Carth took it carefully and slipped it back into her sheath.

"Al-shad was a master of the A'ras," Invar said softly.

Carth's breath caught. She hadn't known. "Felyn killed him so easily!"

He nodded slowly. "That was the first we realized the depths of the threat the Hjan posed. Before that, we knew of them distantly. They were growing in power, but the seat of their power was far from Nyaesh, across the Lhear Sea, so far that our ships could not even reach them. But they reached us."

Carth ran her fingers along the hilt of the knife. "I shouldn't have a master's knife."

"You should have that knife," Invar said.

"Not if he was a master." That somehow made it worse for her. It had been bad enough that she had taken a knife from one of the A'ras, but to claim one of the masters' knives?

"Ms. Rel, I knew Al-shad well. That knife was never his. When you said it was, I thought... the A'ras never reclaimed all of his weapons. But this was not one of them. It is an exquisite blade, but the metal is nothing the A'ras would even use. It does not focus the flame all that well."

"If not his, then whose?" she asked. She had managed to use it to focus the A'ras magic, hadn't she? It worked for more than only the shadows.

Invar shrugged. "If it focuses the shadows for you, perhaps it was your father's."

Carth examined the knife with renewed interest, but there was nothing about it that made her think it could have been his. He had carried knives, but nothing like this. Her father had preferred functional to exotic.

"It couldn't have been his, not where I found it. That's why I thought it belonged to the A'ras when I took it."

"It still could have been his."

"Like I said, not where I found it."

Invar moved toward her, his face showing a burning intensity. "If your father could use the shadows the same way as you, what makes you think he wasn't there?"

Chapter 17

The aged book flipped open to a page Carth couldn't read. She'd tried over the years, searched through the pages as much as she could to try and understand what she might have missed, but understanding came too slowly. The language was not native to her, and as much as she wanted to understand it, she couldn't.

With a sigh, she closed the book again and turned to the next. These had been precious to her parents—her mother, she had always believed—but if she couldn't read them, she would never understand why. There had to be some reason they had hidden them within the wall of the house, and if she understood what that reason might be, she would know if there was any reason for her to hold on to them for so long after her parents were gone. Otherwise, they were empty books, nothing more than memories of her parents.

Could Invar be right? Could her mother not have been from Ih-lash, as Carth had always believed?

Once, Carth would never have believed that, but then, she hadn't known if her father was shadow blessed as well, which he must have been to teach her to use the shadows. Her mother had assisted him, but they had always been her father's games, and her father had always taught the lessons.

What did that make her mother? Was that the reason they had wandered? Carth had never understood—hadn't asked while they still lived, either—but if the shadow born *were* hunted in some way, that would make sense.

Carth tucked the books back into the small cubby next to her bed. She no longer hid them, not as she had when living with Vera, much as she no longer hid the knife. It was funny to her that she might not have needed to hide it; if it wasn't one of the A'ras knives, as she had believed, then could it have been from her father? Was that the reason it seemed to focus her shadows so easily?

She glanced out the window. Too much daylight remained. The days themselves had been odd since the attack, with none of the instructors wanting to spend too much time with the ashai. Carth suspected they felt the need to remain vigilant, which they couldn't do while they were trying to teach.

She needed to get out of her room. Off the palace grounds as well, if she were honest with herself. Once again, the walls felt confining, even though in the aftermath of the attack, she wasn't as confined as she once would have been.

Taking the knife and little else, Carth left her room and made her way into the yard. None of the other students risked coming this close to the wall, giving Carth a measure of peace. Out here, she thought it would take only a brief climb up the wall and she could kick over, reaching the other side, where she could... what? Search for the Hjan on her own? Try to find the shadow born that Invar had brought to the grounds? She'd already proven herself incapable of the latter, and she feared attempting the former.

Carth walked along the perimeter of the wall. For most of it, the ivy grew stout, the long, occasionally thick vines rising along the wall, clinging to it and leaving a dappled shadow upon it. As she reached the area where the Hjan had recently attacked, the ivy simply ended. No shadows curled along the wall created by the shade from the plant. Strangely, here, her connection to the shadows increased.

The replaced stones looked too bright, and the magic used in laying them burned too strongly within her, almost as if the masters had wanted to make up for the fact that the wall had fallen in the first place.

Carth touched the stone with the hand that had been burned. It pulsed softly, making her aware of the magic within the wall as much as of the injury to her hand. She'd taken to wearing a glove on the hand, wanting to shield herself from the annoyance of the way even the gentlest of breezes irritated her skin.

The shadows pulled on her here, more than they had before. The wall that had done little to slow the Hjan had limited her ability with the shadows, but now that it was repaired, there was less of an influence, much less than had been there before.

Touching a hand to the hilt of her knife, she pulled on the shadows.

"You're doing it again."

Carth turned and saw Samis near a row of shrubs, watching her. Those that had been damaged in the attack had been replaced already, the loose soil around them the only sign that there had been any damage.

"Are you following me?"

"Not following. Watching. Thought you might be interesting to keep an eye on."

Carth turned away, releasing the shadows. Instead, she started reaching for the connection to the A'ras magic, letting it slowly flow through her. What if Invar was right and the fact that she used this knife as focus was the reason she wasn't able to pull on the magic easily?

"Listen," Samis said as he ran up to her, jogging backward so that he could see her as he did, "I'm not blaming you for what you did. Sounds like if you hadn't done anything, the attack would have been much worse. The other A'ras there think the masters pressed back the attack, but I saw Master Lyanna's face when she overheard one of them talking. The masters didn't keep the Hjan back, did they?"

"You and Invar are the only ones who know what happened."

"You didn't tell Alison?"

Carth squeezed her eyes shut. As much as she wanted to share with her friend, telling Alison felt dangerous. What would she be able to do to help her? And knowing might only put her at more risk and force her to lie on Carth's behalf. Carth wasn't interested in putting her friend in danger.

"You didn't. I'm not going to say anything," Samis said. He looked at the wall and then back at her. "You know that some of the masters blame the Reshian for the attack?"

"It wasn't the Reshian."

Samis shrugged. "Maybe not. Harrison seems to think it was."

Carth wondered why. What was it that made Harrison believe the Reshian would be capable of what they described? Why would he fear them enough to blame them for this?

"Can you feel them now?" Samis asked.

She nodded. "It's like the first attack. The wall made it impossible to reach the shadows, but now that it's been damaged, I can reach them again."

"Weird that it doesn't keep out the Hjan but does keep out the shadows, isn't it?"

Carth pulled on the sense of the shadows, wrapping the knife in it before releasing it. The effort required to reach the shadows was much greater than on the other side of the wall, but not like what it had been before. Then, she hadn't been able to reach the shadows at all.

Samis looked past her and his eyes widened. "Looks like someone else wants to speak with you."

Carth followed the direction of his gaze. Standing near the wall, where the ivy started to grow, was Invar. He wore his light gray cloak with a sash wrapped around his waist.

"Good luck, Rel."

Samis hurried off, and Carth watched him go. How had she thought that he was such a… a *pain*… for all these years? He had been mostly decent to her here. Alison would hate that she was spending as much time with Samis as she was. If it were up to Alison, she would have been married to Samis a year ago.

Carth approached Invar slowly but remained near the section of the wall without the ivy. At least here, she could still feel the pull of the shadows and could use them if needed.

"Are you ready?" Invar asked.

"For what?"

"We need to continue working on your training, I think."

"Aren't you more concerned about the Hjan?"

"Concerned—yes. But there is little I can do about them other than prepare, and you are a part of those preparations now, Ms. Rel. Now, if you would prefer to remain behind the walls—or maybe you would rather return to the other lessons?"

Neither appealed to her, and she suspected he knew it. "Where are we going today?"

Invar shrugged. "Wandering, I think."

With a surge of power, he leaped over the wall.

Any other time, Carth would have laughed, but the suddenness of what Invar had done wasn't so much amusing as startling.

The only way she would escape the yard would be with the shadows. Using the knife as a focus, she climbed the edge of the ivy and jumped over the wall, kicking through the remaining barrier that held her out.

Invar waited on the other side and seemed unsurprised

when she landed next to him. "I admit I was surprised to learn that you could get past the barrier, Ms. Rel. Now that the wall is even more damaged, I don't think it will keep you out of the city anymore, which means the protections offered by the wall are no longer. You must learn to defend yourself."

"I've sparred plenty of times."

"This will be different than sparring. You have shown yourself capable with the Hjan, perhaps more so than masters can claim. But the Hjan are nothing if not adept at changing, so you must be ready. You must prepare."

"I only did what I had to do."

"And you have been lucky that you've survived to this point. I would have you skilled rather than lucky."

"You know the magic doesn't come for me as well as it does for others."

Invar paused as he strode through the street and dipped his hand into his pocket, pulling out a knife. He handed it to her, hilt first.

It was similar to the one she'd carried for the last five years, but there were differences as well. The metal of the blade had a brighter sheen, almost a purple rather than a deep, silvery gray. The tip curved slightly, and serrations lined the outer edge of the blade. The weighting was the same, and the hilt felt much the same.

"What is this?"

"A knife, Ms. Rel."

She glared at him. "I see that. I have a knife."

"I thought the same, and thought that your difficulty

with pulling the power of the flame came from within you, but I am no longer certain. This knife can be your focus. It is A'ras-made, and done so by a skilled artisan."

"Who?"

He flashed a brief smile. "Me."

Her breath caught as she studied the blade. The masters were skilled with A'ras magic, and they used that to create their swords and knives, making them incredible tools, and incredibly dangerous. Few other than the masters possessed such a weapon.

"I considered a sword, but seeing as you are partial to knives, I thought it made the most sense to create something you are familiar with. The blade is shaped the way it is by necessity, but the hilt and the weighting were designed to feel... familiar."

"It's amazing. I don't think I'm deserving of it."

Invar's face turned serious. "You saved my life, Ms. Rel. Probably twice, considering I doubt I would have made it away from the last attack alive if not for whatever you did. For that, I owe you more than a simple knife can repay. Take it as a token of my appreciation. More than that, take it and see if you can use your potential more effectively through it."

She squeezed the hilt of the knife more firmly and used it as she did to focus her magic. Holding her breath, she reached for the A'ras magic and let it slowly flow through her.

Carth had a flicker of hope that a different knife would make it easier to reach the A'ras magic, that by using Invar's knife, she would somehow find an easier way—one that didn't require the same pain as she currently experienced.

That wasn't the case.

Using this knife for her focus allowed her to reach her magic, but it didn't come any more quickly than it had when using the knife that might or might not have been her father's.

She lowered it, disappointment filling her.

"It doesn't seem to matter. The knife doesn't help any more than the other one did."

Invar rubbed his hands together. "That is... disappointing."

She handed the knife to him, but he shook his head.

"You keep it, Ms. Rel. Even if it does nothing to help you reach your potential any faster, you may still keep it."

He continued along the street while Carth debated what to do with the knife. It was a nice blade, and if made by Invar, it would be valuable as well, but there was something familiar about using the one she'd found those years before. Carth tucked the gift carefully into her belt.

The streetscape changed slowly, and Carth began to recognize where Invar led her. It was the same direction she'd gone with Samis a few nights ago.

"What do you want to do in this part of the city?" she asked.

"You found one of the Hjan where you lived, the last time. I thought it made sense to see if you find something similar in the other places you used to frequent."

They reached the River Road, coming at it from a different direction than she was accustomed. This part of the street had a line of low warehouses. It was where Carth had thought that the A'ras attacked Jhon, and where she had helped protect him. That had been the beginning of her learning about her abilities, the first time he had shared with her that she was more than what she realized.

Invar saw her staring at the warehouses and frowned. "You lived here?" he asked.

Carth nodded. "The tavern down there. The Wounded Lyre. They took me in when my parents were killed."

"What did they ask of you?"

"Nothing. Vera asked that I help sell some of her food and crafts, but there was never any real expectation that I sell a certain amount. She was more motherly than anything."

Invar paused near the tavern. Carth feared that he would want to enter, and that he would reveal her to Vera and Hal, but he didn't, continuing along the street as well. Others on the street parted for them, giving Invar a wide berth. They wouldn't have done the same for her, but she often failed to wear her sash.

He stopped along the shore of the river. Water rushed past, flowing with so much force that spray splashed up and splattered her even where she stood. Firsthand experience told her how fast the current could be, and she had foolishly swum it twice. Had she not spent two summers along the coast of Poi, she doubted she would have been such a good swimmer. Even the children there managed to swim through choppy water, needing to learn so that they could fish.

"Do you sense anything, Ms. Rel?"

She shook her head. "Nothing."

The answer seemed to placate him. "Avera tells me there was a place near here that Felyn used."

Carth pointed along the road, where it wound along the river before eventually stopping. From there, they would have to climb over the rocks to get any farther. After seeing the way the Hjan flickered, she wondered if they would have the same difficulty.

"Do you know that when the masters came to see it, the building was destroyed?" he asked.

"I never went back."

"And you shouldn't have. Strange that Felyn would have died, yet the building fell as well. Who would have known how to bring it down?"

"Avera," she started. Jhon as well, though Carth didn't know enough about what he wanted to know, or whether he would have cared about the building remaining standing. He had helped her, and had helped Avera, but had that been for his benefit or for hers?

"Hmm."

"What do you expect to find down here?" she asked him.

Invar stared over the water. "I don't think that I will find anything, Ms. Rel. I am pleased to know that you don't detect anything either. That tells me the Hjan are gone, for now."

"Or that they don't flicker," she said.

Invar turned back to her, the frown deepening. "What?"

"I don't know if I detect the Hjan, or if I detect the flickering."

Invar's eyes widened slightly. "You raise an interesting

170

question." He turned back to the river, staring out at it.

With the rushing of water, Carth felt a strange sense of peace, in spite of knowing that there was a dangerous threat roaming the city and that she might be the only one able to detect it. She still didn't know if that had anything to do with the shadow blessing, or if there was something else different about her. A part of her wished she could jump into the river, let it carry her downstream and away from the city, but she could not. Her responsibility was to this place now.

"Ms. Rel," Invar said without turning back to her, "I think it is time that you begin patrolling with others."

"Patrols?" she asked dumbly.

"Your ability allows you to detect things that others cannot."

"But I'm still so slow at reaching my potential."

"Perhaps slow, but not weak. You have shown that you have much talent. Besides, you are not reliant only upon your A'ras potential."

"What does that mean?"

Invar turned to her and his gaze drifted to the knife at her waist before he reached into his pocket and pulled out a sash wider than the one she wore, but narrower than Invar's. "It means, Ms. Rel, that I am raising you to sai."

Chapter 18

The change came immediately.

As Carth wore the sash onto the palace grounds, whispering followed her. This time, the whispers were for different reasons from what she'd ever experienced. She heard her name, and the word *sai*, mixed with the occasional mention of Master Invar.

She hurried to her room in the cosak, only to find Alison already waiting for her.

She looked at the sash tied around Carth's arm. It felt strange wearing one so wide, and she was tempted to fold it up—going so far as to actually have folded it up initially, only to have Invar tell her that she should not.

"So it's true," Alison said.

Carth glanced at her arm, still uncertain what to make of it. She didn't feel she deserved the promotion—she certainly hadn't done anything to earn it—but since one of the masters had given it to her, who was she to decline?

"I guess," Carth said.

Alison snorted and dropped onto Carth's bed. "You

guess. You could at least act happy about it. You're nearly A'ras now!" Alison looked around her room, turning her nose up slightly. "What was your test?"

"Test?"

She bobbed her head. "Yes, test. There's always a test to get past ashai. What did you have to do?"

Carth thought about what Invar had asked of her while they had made their way through the city, but couldn't come up with anything. He had given her the knife and asked her to try to summon power using it as a focus, but she hadn't managed that any better than she normally did. And he hadn't asked her to hold on to the magic as they made their way through the street, not as he had the first time they'd left the palace.

"There wasn't a test," she said.

Alison arched a brow at her. "There's *always* a test, Carthenne Rel."

She shook her head. "I think he only raised me so that I could get out on patrols. He wants me in the city so that I can detect if the Hjan return."

"That's no reason for him to raise you. He could take you himself like he did before."

"He's only taken me out of the city twice since working with me."

"That's twice more than I've been out," Alison said. "At least you've been out in the actual city twice."

"More than that," Carth admitted. When Alison shot her a look, she explained how she'd chased the man from Ihlash. Carth hated keeping things from her closest friend.

"Maybe that's why he raised you. If the wall doesn't create any barrier for you, better to have you controlled when you leave."

Carth looked away. It stung having Alison think the same things. In some ways, it was fine for her to have thoughts about herself and believe that she shouldn't be raised to the sai. It was another for her closest friend to have the same thoughts.

"I don't know. As I said, I don't know why he raised me."

"At least this way you get out from these walls, even if you still can't reach your magic that well."

Carth squeezed her eyes closed. "I only stopped back here for something. I have to get back—"

Alison hopped off her bed. "I'm glad for you, Carthenne. It tells me that if you can do it, I can do it, too!"

Carth only nodded. "I… I'm going to change. Why don't I find you later?"

Alison smiled, somehow completely seeming to miss the fact that her words hurt—that it would be Alison who would do that cut Carth more than if anyone else had.

After Alison left, Carth closed the door and leaned on it. She reached for the sash and considered tearing it off. What *had* she done to deserve to wear it? Nothing. Even the newest of the ashai could reach their potential faster than her. Was the only reason Invar had raised her because she managed to wound the Hjan? Was that reason enough to elevated her above so many others?

Carth didn't think it was her sense of the Hjan. It was only because of her other ability. Carth felt more and more certain of that.

A knock on the door startled her and she pulled it open, expecting Alison, hoping that she'd realized what she'd said and how it had affected Carth. Instead, she found Samis. Much like Alison, his gaze dropped to the sash and his eyes widened.

"You heard."

He smiled, waiting for her to open the door for him. Reluctantly, Carth pulled it open and let him in. Samis would only force himself in otherwise, but at least now he didn't outrank her. "I think the entire cosak heard, Rel. Congrats."

Carth waited for some sarcastic comment, something that would be in line with what Alison had said, but he wore an earnest expression.

"Thanks."

"Can't say I'm surprised."

"Why—because I can use the shadows? You think that's the only reason I'd get raised to sai?"

Samis held his hands out to her, palms facing her. "Whoa! I don't know what set you off, but I'm not telling you anything you don't already know. I've sparred with you, Rel. I've seen how strong you are. You have talent. If you were any faster, you would have beat me the last time we sparred." He managed to say it without making it sound like he was boasting. "I'm not surprised the Aren raised you."

"It wasn't the Aren," Carth said.

"What? All the ashai go before the Aren before they're elevated. The only other way you can be elevated is…" His breath caught. "Oh. No one has been raised that way in years."

Carth swallowed. "I know the history."

Samis nodded. "I suppose you do. So it was Master Invar?"

She ran her fingers along the scarf, tracing the smooth silk. "Invar," she agreed.

"You know that he has never raised anyone before? The other masters have all had favorites they've raised, but not him. Maybe you're his favorite now."

She unsheathed the knife and showed it to Samis. She hadn't any interest in sharing with Alison. "He *did* give me a knife," she said.

Samis took the knife and traced his fingers over it. "Master Invar gave this to you?"

When she nodded, he whistled softly. A brief pulse of power came from him, enough for her to know that he used the knife to focus his potential. His eyes widened and he released the magic. "Wow. This is... this is an impressive blade, Rel. With something like this, you should be able to reach for your ability even faster."

"That's what Invar said."

Samis looked up from studying the blade and handed it back over to her. "Didn't work?"

She sighed. "Not like he had hoped. There's something different about the way I use my magic. It's not the focus, Samis, it's *me*."

Samis laughed and Carth shot him a hard look. He shrugged. "Of course it's you. You have this ability with the shadows, one that's not like what I can do. The mixture has to do something to your ability to reach the A'ras magic."

Carth sighed, taking the knife back from him. Samis held on to it for a moment, flashing a smile as he did, before releasing it. Her other hand went to her mother's ring she kept on a necklace, clutching it beneath her shirt. "I just wish it was easier for me."

He laughed, and she found herself laughing along with him. "Of course you do, Rel. We all want it to be easier, but what's worthwhile is never easy."

She arched her brow at him. "Now you're getting philosophical with me?"

"Naw, just something my father used to say. Of course, that was mostly when I told him I was scared about how hard it was going to be when I got here."

"What do you mean, *got here*? You're from Nyaesh. I've heard you say it."

Samis shrugged. "I'm not from the city, Rel. My parents own land near the border with Holyth. I hadn't been to the city until I came to study."

"I don't understand. How did you know you had the potential?"

"I didn't think I would. The A'ras make a sweep through all the villages once a year looking for those with the potential. You make it to A'ras—and I don't have any reason to think you won't—you'll probably have to make a pass as well. They came through looking for those with potential and found me. I... well, let's just say I wasn't all that excited at the time."

"You didn't want to come study with the A'ras?"

His face soured. "Didn't you hear me say it was hard? My

father owned land, we had servants, so I had an *easy* life, Rel. This… this is nothing like what I experienced."

"But you're so skilled!"

He shrugged again. "I never wanted to be skilled. I didn't try when I first came here. That was before your time, so you wouldn't have known, but I wasn't always the best ashai student. The masters threatened to send me back nearly a dozen times. Back then, I *wanted* to return."

Carth tried thinking of Samis as lazy. Since she'd come to study with the A'ras, he had been nothing but one of the hardest workers, and one of the best students. "What changed?"

"Me, I suppose. I had no choice but to change."

"Why? Couldn't you have gone back to your land and your servants and the easy way of life?"

"Maybe once, but Holyth claimed our land. Killed some of my father's men. Nearly killed my family. I don't have land I can go back to anymore."

He fell silent, and Carth didn't know what to say. "I'm sorry, Samis."

Samis played with his hands, twisting his fingers together. "Worst part of all of this? I tell myself that, had I not been here, I could have helped. Then I tell myself that if I learn all I can, I can help my father claim his lands again, even when I know—I *know*—the A'ras won't allow the magic to be used in that way. Wait… that wasn't the worst part. No, that was hearing from a letter—and from my sister—that we'd lost our land. Our home. People who'd served the family for generations."

He swallowed and took a shaky breath. "I shouldn't be telling you any of this. I don't want to burden you, Rel. I know you've been through your own shit."

She sat on her bed and waited for him to sit next to her. "My mother was killed over five years ago. I thought the A'ras killed her and learned later that it was the Hjan. She... I was supposed to be with her, but I didn't keep up." It was the thing she didn't dare share with anyone else, the fear that she should have been there, that there might have been something she could have done, even though she had known nothing of her abilities then. Had she been there, she would have died too. "My father... I don't know what happened to him. I never saw him again. I heard them talking, though, and knew that they went after him. Had it not been for Vera..."

Samis took her hand, and she didn't resist. She felt vulnerable and scared, but not because she shared with Samis.

"There are things we can't change, Rel. All we can do is learn from the past and work on getting better for the future."

"Still philosophical."

"That was my father, too. That came in the letter from him. It was the only one he ever sent, and he sent it after my sister sent hers. I think he worried I'd try to come home." He swallowed. "Since then, I've pushed myself. I *want* to get better, Rel. I want to do what I can to help. I can't do that without pushing myself."

He stared at his hands for a few minutes more before standing. "Anyway, I'm happy for you, Rel. That's all I wanted to say."

"Thanks." What did it mean that the person most excited for her happened to be the boy she'd spent the last few years annoyed with? Why couldn't her best friend bother to be happy for her and not make her feel worse about what she'd accomplished?

"The lessons get harder, but you start to learn more, too. You think being ashai is difficult, wait until you start some of your sai classes." He smiled, pausing as he reached the door. "Have you gotten your assignment yet?"

She shook her head. "When should I expect it?"

"I don't know. I got mine when the Aren promoted me. That this came from Master Invar… I don't know. Maybe he'll be the one to make the assignment. For your sake, you'd better hope so."

"Why?"

"Not all assignments are the same. I got lucky, and they let me serve with Gabe and Ilyan. They're both pretty decent to new sai. There are some who aren't quite as decent."

Carth hadn't even considered who she might be assigned to patrol with. She'd been so focused on the fact that she'd been granted the promotion that she hadn't stopped to think about what it meant when she actually got to the patrolling.

"I guess you better hope Master Invar chooses."

As he closed the door behind him, Carth wondered what sort of assignment she might get.

Chapter 19

Her assignment came late the next day, leaving Carth wondering through much of the day if she wouldn't get assigned at all for some reason. There was a terrible period where she wondered if Invar had made a mistake, and imagined what the other ashai's response would be if she had to sulk back into the classes. It had been bad enough going back to the ashai classes when Master Invar had disappeared, but for her to be elevated, only to have that taken from her... That would be worse.

Trista delivered the assignment, summoning Carth to the north part of the yard and waiting with the compact man who had helped her bring Invar into the palace. Carth had wondered why she'd been summoned, but she had been careful to put her wider sash on when she left the cosak, not wanting to cause any more gossip than she already did.

"Rel," Trista said sharply when she appeared. "You've been assigned to patrol with Devn and myself."

The assignment wasn't nearly as bad as what she'd worked herself into believing. She'd known Trista and knew her to be reasonable, and while she didn't know Devn, the fact that he worked with Trista made it more likely he would at least be decent.

She smiled, but the smile faded as Trista stared at her. "I don't know what Invar thought, raising you the way he did," Trista said, "but if you think you can talk to me the way you did that day you brought him back to the palace, you're going to find this is an unpleasant assignment."

A flush rolled through her. She hadn't thought it was going to be easy, but she wanted a chance. That was all. "Of course. I'm here to do whatever is needed."

Trista glanced over at Devn. "Hear that, Devn? Whatever is needed."

He shrugged. "We'll see."

"You follow us. Don't say anything, you get that? You're sai. That means you don't talk. Observe. Stay ready. That's it."

Carth nodded, unprepared for the hostility from Trista, who led them to the gate, guiding them into the city. Carth reached for her connection to the A'ras magic, tearing it through her veins so that she would be ready for whatever might come. She didn't have to do anything with it, only hold on to it, keep it burning within her at a low level. For now, that was enough.

When she crossed through the gate, Carth immediately reached for the shadows as well. She held on to this, mixing it with her steadily burning connection to the A'ras, and let it fill her. Strangely, the sense of shadows restored her, whereas using the A'ras magic did nothing but make her tired.

Trista and Devn spoke softly to each other as they marched into the city. Much as people had with Invar, they parted around Trista and Devn, though it seemed like that had as much to do with the fact that they so openly wore their sashes, almost as if making a point of showing that they were A'ras.

They weaved in a circle around the palace before starting on another circle. By the third, Carth couldn't stand it anymore and spoke up. "Are we assigned to make circles?"

Devn glanced at her and looked away, but Trista glared openly. "I thought I told you that you weren't to challenge me. Wasn't that the deal, Devn?"

"That was what you said, Trista."

"See? That's what I said. We're on patrol. The A'ras guide the patrol, and not the sai. If you think you want to lead, then you'll have to wait until you can convince one of the masters to raise you to A'ras, though that *is* a little harder to convince them of."

"I didn't ask him to raise me."

Trista leaned toward her. "Did you want to argue with me, Rel?"

Arguing wouldn't get her anywhere and might even lead to her getting reassigned. She didn't want that, but she didn't want to be treated like this, either. "Not argue. I only wondered if there was a reason we're wandering in circles."

"Do you think you know the city better than us? You've barely been raised from ashai. All that time behind the walls make you think you somehow know the city better than you do?"

Carth bit back the retort that came to mind. She might know the city as well as Trista. The time she'd spent collecting scraps had allowed her the chance to wander, and she'd discovered places in the city that she doubted any of the A'ras knew. They were places where the A'ras wouldn't be allowed—her now as well.

"I'll follow wherever you want to go," she said, forcing meekness into her voice.

Trista stared at her a moment, her hand gripping her knife as if she wanted Carth to challenge her, before turning back to Devn and starting along the street. She didn't say anything more to Carth, dismissing her.

They continued to make slow spirals through the city, steadily moving farther from the palace and the yard. Carth held on to the A'ras magic, but also to the shadows flowing around her, hoping she didn't detect anything that would make her think the Hjan had returned. Trista wouldn't take well to that.

By the time they reached a small square—one that reminded Carth of her mother's death—she had given up on the idea that they would find anything. And maybe that was what patrols were all about. That was something she really should have asked Samis about when he had been willing to discuss the assignments.

Trista stopped, pulled a bottle of water out from beneath her robe, and took a long sip of it. Devn did the same. Carth hadn't known to bring water—and hadn't brought any food, either—so stood watching.

As she did, she noticed a strange humming. It started

slowly, building steadily until it was unmistakable. She watched Trista and Devn, but neither gave any sign that they detected it.

After a while, she couldn't take it anymore. "What is that?" she asked.

Devn turned to her, but Trista was the one who answered. "What are you talking about, Rel?"

"The buzzing sound. Don't you hear it?"

Trista and Devn met each other's eyes and grinned. "Already?" Devn asked.

"Already what?" Carth asked, stepping toward them. She grew tired of them ignoring her, or treating her like she couldn't ask questions. How else was she going to learn what was expected of her?

"Not surprised that it happened so soon," Trista said. "Think about what she claims happened to Master Invar."

"Invar's been getting senile. The others know it, but they allow him to remain because of what he's done for the A'ras."

"This might be the worst of it," Trista went on. "The man has never raised any to sai and now he chooses *her*?"

Devn shrugged. "The right of the masters, I suppose. Doesn't mean she'll make it to A'ras."

Carth stepped forward, and the sound shifted.

It didn't come from all around any longer; now there was a direction to it. East.

Toward the palace.

Carth turned and started toward it. The buzzing wasn't a steady sound, as she had first believed. This came with a sort of fluctuating sense and wasn't so much a sound as a feeling, much like she felt A'ras magic when used, only this wasn't painful.

"Rel?" Trista asked.

The sound shifted again. Carth didn't want to answer and risk losing the connection to the sound. She went into an alley, leaving the square.

"Rel!"

Carth knew she should go back, but what if this was some new trick of the Hjan?

She started running, focusing on the sense of the buzzing as she did and losing the connection to the A'ras magic. Rather than trying to regain it, she shifted that minimal attention to the shadows and, without really meaning to, cloaked herself in them.

The buzzing continued, but cloaked as she was, it became easier for her to focus on the buzzing, and now it practically vibrated within her.

Carth hurried faster. She'd never felt anything like this before. Could it be the Hjan?

Invar suspected they were after something, but he hadn't shared with her what he feared. She wasn't even A'ras, but didn't she deserve a little more information, especially considering all she'd done to stop the Hjan so far?

At the wall, she expected to find damage, or begin feeling the distinctive nausea that came from the Hjan, but there was nothing, only the steady buzzing.

Carth drifted along the wall, holding on to the shadows, holding on to the cloak, worried she might find one of the Hjan and be unprepared.

She found nothing.

Carth slipped forward and touched the wall. Had it always vibrated like it did now?

No—that was new. Not A'ras, though. And not Hjan.

What was it?

Another attack.

Carth ran around the perimeter of the palace wall, maintaining her hold on the shadows and touching her fingers to the wall as she did. The vibration remained. At the damaged sections, she actually felt it more acutely, as if whatever caused the vibration remained within the stone. She wasn't able to determine if it weakened the walls.

Reaching her starting place, she almost jumped the wall to return and try to find Invar when another sense came to her.

It wasn't only the wall that carried with it the vibration.

Carth moved slowly, searching for another sign of what she detected. It was faint but growing steadily stronger. Whatever caused it was happening now. She eased her hold on the shadows, but that made the sound harder to detect, so she increased her hold once more, pulling more strongly upon the shadows, tightening the cloak around her.

As she did, the steady buzzing became something else: a hum of energy.

Magic.

That was what she detected, and different than A'ras magic, different even than her shadow magic.

It ran along the street, traces of it that ran in a straight line away from the palace. Not only one line, but several, like spokes on a wheel, each leading away from the palace. Carth picked up on one of the lines and started following. She kept herself mixed in the shadows as she went, holding the connection so that she could follow the hum of energy more easily. The trail led her down Doland Street. Carth should have been surprised by that, but she wasn't. The hum centered on the street, and she followed it as it radiated away from the palace grounds, eventually fading near the docks.

Once in the streets below, she froze, looking around.

Dozens of people moved, unaware that she was there. She saw nothing else that suggested there were other practitioners of magic nearby. The hum had faded, and the buzzing hadn't returned. Whatever she'd detected near the palace wasn't present here.

As she turned back toward the palace, she saw a familiar face.

He was older now—much like her—and his once smiling face had been replaced by a serious mask, but it was still Kel.

For a moment, she considered releasing the shadows and going to him but decided against it. What would that serve, other than to make her feel worse? She'd said her goodbye, left him where he could be safe.

This wasn't her home anymore, if it ever had been.

Turning back up the street, she made her way toward the palace. With each step, she expected the hum of energy to return, but it didn't. By the time she reached the palace, she'd almost convinced herself that she'd imagined it. She needed to find Invar and tell him what she had sensed. He might be the only one who would believe her. And she would need to find out how upset Trista and Devn would be that she'd abandoned them on patrol. This wasn't an auspicious start to her first day as sai.

Chapter 20

Master Invar paced in front of Carth, restrained anger seething off of him. Carth sat quietly, hands crossed in her lap, her eyes focused straight ahead on the tapestry hanging from the wall. She didn't want to set him off any more than he already was.

"You ran off yesterday, Ms. Rel. You had an assignment, and you ran off."

She hadn't been able to find him until today, and she feared returning to Trista and Devn until she did. "I didn't run off. I told you—"

He turned toward her. "You were given an assignment, Ms. Rel."

"Don't you even want to know what I detected?"

"There was nothing you could have detected."

She stood, irritated, and scanned his room. Invar had summoned her to his personal quarters rather than the Master Hall, and rather than finding her outside the palace. In some ways, that troubled her more.

The one person she needed to understand what she'd

sensed because he had been the one person who had seemed to understand refused to listen to her. It was bad enough that it had taken her until morning to find him, and that when she had found him, he had seemed more annoyed than interested in what she had to tell him. "Didn't you feel it? There was a buzzing of energy. I didn't know it was energy until I reached the palace wall, but I could feel it vibrating within the wall! But it wasn't only the wall, it was along the streets, spreading out all around the palace. Master Invar, you have to believe—"

He turned to her, and his eyes wore a flat expression. "You should not have been able to detect that."

Carth blinked. "You knew?"

He waved a hand at her. "Of course I knew, Ms. Rel. Why do you think the protection was placed? The A'ras flame has not been enough; the Hjan treat it like there's nothing to it. We needed additional protections."

"That... that wasn't the Hjan?"

"Did you feel the nausea?"

"Well, no. But I didn't know if that was because they weren't flickering."

"They call it traveling, Ms. Rel. If you're going to study them, it would be best if you used the appropriate term."

"I don't want to study them. I want to be safe when they attack."

Invar sniffed. "Safe. When the Hjan attack, you've seen that there's no real safety. The only person who I've ever witnessed able to make a difference when they attack is you." He rubbed his hand across his head, and power briefly surged from him. "What did you feel?"

"I told you what I felt. It was a buzzing. It started softly, but it became more intense the longer I detected it. It was most prominent near the palace, all the way around the wall."

"Do you still detect it?"

She shook her head. The buzzing had been gone when she'd returned from chasing the strand through the street toward the dock. "Is it gone?"

"Not gone. I have added another layer atop it to conceal it."

Would she have detected another layer on top of the buzzing? She hadn't focused on it, but was that possible?

"What is the buzzing?" she asked him. "If it's not A'ras, and it's not Hjan, what is it?"

"You have already learned that there are other kinds of power in the world, Ms. Rel."

"Like the Hjan."

"The Hjan are one extreme example, but theirs is unique in a way. They don't possess their power naturally, not as you and I do."

"How do they get it, then?"

"They study power, find ways to borrow it. Some have minimal abilities that they augment, like we use the knives and swords to augment our power."

"And the Ih-lash?"

"I'm afraid I am not the right person to ask about the Ih-lash," he said. "They have always been secretive, as you can imagine."

"You found Jicanl. You must know something."

"I didn't find him. I went looking for others who would be able to provide me with information."

"What others?"

Invar sighed. "There are others who study power, Ms. Rel. In some ways, they are like the Hjan. They study power, learn from it, but they don't attempt to use it the same way. They prefer knowledge of natural powers, that of plants, and of metals and colors, all that they use to add to abilities they already possess."

"And Jicanl was one of them?"

"These others put me in contact with him, yes."

"Are they the ones who placed the buzzing magic around the palace?"

He nodded. "They are."

"And you didn't expect me to detect what they did."

"As I've said, Ms. Rel, your ability to detect magical presence is like nothing I have ever experienced."

"Why? Why can I detect other magic when others can't?"

Invar shook his head. "I don't know that I'll be able to offer you a satisfactory answer. Perhaps it is the shadows that grant you that ability, or perhaps it is the fact that you have lived in other places, places with power of their own. When it was only the A'ras and the Hjan, I thought I might be able to explain it, but you should not also be able to detect this power. None of the A'ras can do that."

What did that make her? If she could detect magic that even the masters weren't able to detect, what did that mean for her?

Carth had wanted only to have a home, to be welcomed, but the longer she was here, the more she learned she could do what others could not, she felt distanced.

Invar seemed to sense the concern within her and took a seat next to her, patting her on the arm. "You have the potential to be powerful within the A'ras, Ms. Rel. That is the reason that I chose for you to be sai. The Aren do not always see beyond the basic skills. You might not be the fastest, and you might still be raw, but there is much strength in you."

"You didn't only raise me because I can detect the Hjan?"

Invar tilted his head as he eyed her. "Is that what you fear?"

"I don't want to be given something I don't deserve."

"Don't you feel that you deserve what you were given?"

"I don't want to have been given it. I want to have earned my place with the sai."

Invar smiled. "Good. Know that you *have* earned it, Ms. Rel. Others might have a different understanding of what you're capable of doing, but know that I've seen it."

"But only because of what I can do with the Hjan."

"That's not the only reason. Admittedly, that is a part of the reason, and one that I will not apologize for, but it is not the entirety of the reason. You have potential. Whether you reach that potential will be up to you."

She sensed the dismissal and stood, getting ready to leave him. As she reached his door, she paused. "The protection that was placed. You fear another attack on the palace?"

"I fear the Hjan have not abandoned their intended target."

"The information they want."

Invar tipped his head in a slight nod.

"Did it work?"

"We will see, Ms. Rel. Now it is time for you to return to your patrol. I believe A'ras Trista awaits you."

A part of Carth had hoped he would assign her elsewhere, but there was no reason for that. She had her assignment and she needed to keep it, regardless of how frustrated she might be with it.

Invar turned back to the table he'd been working at when she'd first arrived, and she understood the dismissal.

Carth left his room and hurried from the palace. Would she even find Trista and Devn? It might be late enough that they'd left the grounds for the day, and without being with them, she wouldn't be able to get through the gate. She might be able to climb the wall—though she'd have to test whether she still could now that Invar had had additional protections layered on it—but that wasn't the way she should reach her patrol.

Surprisingly, she found Trista and Devn waiting for her at the door to the palace. Trista glared at her, annoyance already brewing within her, and Devn shook his head.

"You will *not* run off from us again, Rel. The next time, I'm reporting you to the Aren."

"Still think she should have been reported this time," Devn said.

Trista shot him a hard look and he fell silent.

"I'm… I'm sorry." Nothing else would ease Trista's irritation with her, so she decided not to try.

Trista slapped her hand on her crossed arms and then turned toward the gate without another word. Devn followed.

As Carth trailed after them, she caught a glimpse of Samis on the other side of the yard. He nodded to her and flashed a smile. How much easier would it be for her to remain as one of the ashai? She could bide her time in lessons, not worrying about offending the A'ras, but she would never have the same permission to leave the yard, to get out into the city where she could reach the shadows and feel the way they cloaked her. For that, she had to sacrifice, and that meant doing what Trista and Devn asked of her.

When they started their patrol—once more making a slow spiral around the city—Carth reached immediately for the shadows. This time, she held on to the connection and ignored the A'ras magic. Using the shadows didn't take the same effort, and the shadows had been more useful to her. Besides, she wanted to learn if there was anything she might discover about the hum of energy, and she thought she'd be better able to manage that using the shadows.

When they neared the square where she'd first detected the buzzing, Devn dropped back. He had deep brown eyes and a sun-darkened face. "What did you detect yesterday, Rel?"

She shook her head. "It was nothing. I shouldn't have gone off without you."

Devn looked up at her. "You must have sensed something. Don't hear about you bolting too often. Most claim you were foolish enough to run *toward* the last attack.

Seems to me you must have picked up on something."

They started along a street that would eventually bring them out of Nyaesh, but Trista didn't move in a direct route, choosing to weave through alleys and veer off on less well-traveled roads. The distant city wall occasionally came into view, but they never seemed to get too close to it, always turning so that they ran parallel to it or at times moved deeper within the city once more. When Trista had claimed she knew the city better than Carth did, she hadn't been lying.

"What was it, Rel?" Trista asked, glancing over her shoulder.

"I don't know. A buzzing sound. Or feeling. It came from the palace, and with the recent attacks…"

Devn looked at Trista. "See? Runs toward trouble. Who does that?"

"We don't even know that there was trouble."

He shrugged. "If there was, and if she ran toward it, can't get too mad at her."

Trista said nothing.

Late in the day, they heard a commotion.

They were nearer the wall than they had been before. The sounds of shouts rang out from an alley. Trista motioned them forward, hand resting on the hilt of her sword as she did.

"Careful here. The damn Reshian think they can assault A'ras."

"Reshian? How can they attack without magic?" Carth asked.

"Don't need magic to cause trouble, do you?" Devn asked, unsheathing his sword. "Enough damage can be done with a sharp blade and skilled hand."

Trista reached the mouth of the alley. Magic burned from her. Carth reached for her knife, debating whether she would use shadow magic if needed, or A'ras.

Devn followed, with Carth behind him. Shadows swallowed them.

Carth didn't have a chance to decide which magic she'd use.

Five men appeared out of the shadows. Holding her cloaking as she did, she could feel them almost parting the shadows. No nausea rolled through her. Not Hjan, then.

Somehow Trista didn't see them. Neither did Devn.

"Watch out!" she shouted.

Carth reached for her shadow blessing, pulling it around her as she spun with the knife, catching the blade of the man nearest Trista as he attacked. She managed to turn it and kicked, sending him flying backward. Carth spun, grabbing the wrist of the next man before he could reach Devn, and snapping it.

Trista and Devn surged into action. Their magic flowed, burning beneath Carth's skin, leaving it tight. Devn in particular was impressive. His sword flashed with such speed, and with such power drawn from his magic, that Carth almost hesitated.

That would have been deadly.

Another three emerged from deeper in the alley.

Carth detected them through the shadows. She doubted she would have otherwise. They slipped forward and would have caught Trista in the back were it not for Carth recognizing that they had appeared.

She cloaked herself in the shadows.

Knifing forward, she reached the nearest man and caught him with her blade. He fell, and the others converged on her, somehow able to detect her in spite of the shadows.

Carth tore at the darkness around them, dragging it to her. As she did, she kicked, catching the nearest man in the leg, and he crumpled. The other spun toward her, leaping in the air as he did. Carth sliced, swinging her blade so that she caught him in the thigh, leaving him hobbled. Another kick, and he fell.

It only took another moment to finish the others.

When she was done, Trista eyed Carth. "You saw them?"

"I heard them," she said. How else would she explain that she had known the attack was coming? She doubted Trista would believe her if she said she used the shadows, and after what she'd seen here with the Reshian, she wasn't sure she wanted to share that.

They had used the shadows too. Maybe not in the same way Carth had, but they'd used the shadows.

"What is it, Rel?" Trista asked. "You look like you're going to be sick."

"Happens after a first attack," Devn said. "Maybe we should get her back."

Trista watched her and nodded. "We've got to report anyway."

Carth followed, looking back at the fallen men as they left them there.

"The Aren will send another crew, don't worry," Devn said.

Carth couldn't tell him that wasn't the reason she stared. He wouldn't understand, and she wasn't sure she wanted his understanding. All she could do was nod.

Chapter 21

When Carth returned, she went looking for Samis but didn't find him in the cosak. He'd understand what had happened, even if there was nothing he could have done to help. She found it strange that she didn't go looking for Alison like she once would have.

Instead, Alison caught her in the hall before following her back out of the cosak. As she stood in front of her friend, she realized that she needed to tell Invar what happened. He needed to know that the Reshian had shadow magic, and she wanted to learn if he already knew.

Alison wore her narrow band of maroon around her neck like a scarf, and a pair of knives were sheathed at her waist.

"What happened?" Alison asked. "You look like you're going to be sick. It's not another attack—"

"Not another attack," she told Alison. "Not the Hjan, at least," she clarified.

"You *were* attacked?"

Trista and Devn approached the cosak and nodded curtly. "I'm going to give my report, Rel. Before I do, I wanted to tell you nice work out there. Had you not recognized the threat, we…"

"We would've been dead, Rel. You did good work."

Carth could only nod. It was strange getting praise from them, but then, as the day had gone on, they had slowly warmed to her.

"Pretty sure the Aren aren't going to like what happened there," Trista said as she started away.

"You mean having the Reshian attack us so openly? Yeah, I'm thinking they won't be thrilled."

When they left, Alison turned to her. "You *were* attacked."

Carth nodded. "Attacked, but not the same way you think. This was…" She didn't know what it was, only that there was more to the attacks than what she understood. "I don't know. It's only been my second day, so I don't know what it was. Something, though."

Alison touched the knives at her waist.

"Where were you going?"

"Sparring," Alison said quickly. "If I want to get raised to sai, I need to prove that I'm capable."

"Yeah, because if I can do it, then anyone can."

Carth turned away and started toward the palace. She would find Invar, and then she would discover what he knew about the Reshian and if it had anything to do with the Ihlash.

Alison raced up to her and caught her by the wrist, forcing Carth to turn and face her. "That's not what I meant, and you know it!"

Carth jerked her arm free. "That's what you said."

Alison opened her mouth before clamping it closed again. "That is what I said, isn't it? I'm sorry, Carthenne Rel. I know that you're talented, just as I know that you deserve to get raised to the sai."

Carth took a deep breath. Alison waited, her face pensive, and Carth knew that she couldn't stay mad at her closest friend. She'd need her as she tried to figure out what she was meant to do, and she'd need her friend's support. Alison had been her constant friend. Losing her now, and for a stupid reason like this... that would hurt more than anything else.

"It took me long enough," she said, forcing a smile.

Alison let out a relieved breath and reached to hug her. Carth let her pull her close, thinking of all the times Alison had comforted her over the years. "Only because you didn't try before."

"I'm still not trying," Carth said. "Invar makes me, even if I don't want to."

"How dare he see in you what I've seen all along!"

Carth sighed. It felt right having Alison back supporting her, but she couldn't stay here. "I have to find Invar," she said.

"For your lessons? I thought he wouldn't continue them now that you're sai. You'd have different lessons."

Carth hadn't asked, but maybe Alison was right. Maybe Invar wouldn't continue to teach her now that she had been raised. "That, and there's something else."

Alison's face fell slightly when Carth didn't offer anything more. She couldn't, not until she understood what she had seen. "Find me later?" Alison asked.

Carth nodded. She hurried across the grounds until she came to the palace. The pair of A'ras who stood guard at the door let her in without question. Once inside, she hurried to the Master Hall and knocked, but no one answered. She tried Invar's room, thinking he might be there if anywhere, but that was empty as well.

Returning to the main door, she stopped. "Have you seen Master Invar?" Carth asked.

Rond, a slender A'ras who had to be at least ten years older than her, shook his head. "Master hasn't been here most of the day."

"Do you know when he might return?"

"The masters don't provide us with a schedule, Rel."

Carth sighed and left the palace. She wandered across the yard slowly. She could do as Alison asked and return to her, but Carth wanted to talk to someone about what she'd seen, and Alison wouldn't understand the significance. Recognizing that pained her.

"Rel."

Carth turned and saw Samis near a cluster of trees, watching her. She let out a relieved breath. She might not be able to share with Invar, but Samis should understand. "Samis."

He smiled as he stepped away from the trees. "I heard you can't keep yourself from excitement. The others seem to think you're a magnet for it."

Carth blanched. If that was the case...

"Don't worry. I don't think you're all *that* bad."

"We were attacked by Reshian."

"Really? We haven't seen any traces in the city. They're supposed to be here, but we've never come across any. Rumors outside, though."

She leaned closer to him. "They were using the shadows, Samis."

"Are you sure?"

"I didn't want to believe it, but that's the only thing that makes sense. They shrouded themselves before they attacked. They nearly got to Trista."

Samis whistled. "Good thing you were there. Good thing you always seem to be there when this sort of thing happens."

Carth hated that he was right. Not only with the Hjan, but with the strange humming energy she'd detected, and now with this attack. What did it mean for her that she was always where the attacks came? Could she draw them toward her?

"Rel... I see what you're thinking. This isn't on you. The Reshian have been making their way into the city for the last few weeks. There's nothing about what you do that puts us at more risk."

Weeks. "Ever since the Hjan attacks," Carth said.

Samis shrugged. "I don't think they're the same. You know the Reshian have been here for much longer than the Hjan."

"I don't know anything about them, really. Only that they tried abducting some of the kids along the docks when I lived there."

Samis nodded. "Slave trade. They're a part of that. Kids are easiest to move, part of the reason we're brought into the palace grounds when we train. They like taking women, too. My sister was almost snatched on the trip to Nyaesh."

"Why women?"

Samis frowned. "Are you asking a serious question? Women for prostitution. There's a market in the southlands, though it's mostly across the Lhear Sea. Not much of that here. Not much of the slave trade here, either." He smiled. "We're a bit more refined."

"We should do something to stop it!"

"You want the A'ras to climb onto ships and cross the sea so that we can prevent slavery? I think we've got enough trouble within Nyaesh, Carth. We've got magic, but it's not as strong as what others possess. The Hjan attacks have shown us that. We can fight, but there are others with as much skill. My father always told me about a place called Neeland, where the swordsmen are deadly. What do we have that other places don't?"

"When I was younger, my family moved around a lot. We never found anything like what you're describing."

"Like I said, we've got our own problems. These are violent lands, with enough fighting that it spills over to other places, but we don't have the same slavery issue they have in the south. Trade one for another, I guess."

"Like the Reshian."

"The Reshian. They're bad, Carth. They aren't afraid to make the crossing. They have skilled captains, and skilled fighters."

"And they can use the shadows."

Samis sighed. "If they can, then that's even more reason to be careful. Listen to what Trista has you do. She's a skilled A'ras."

"I plan on telling Invar."

"Good, but you should know Master Invar doesn't have the same reputation he once did. Some are thinking that his mind is going."

"I've not seen anything that would tell me his mind is slipping," Carth said.

"Would you know?"

"I think I've spent enough time with him the last few weeks to have recognized it, so yes."

Samis shrugged. "You might be the only one who feels that way, at least from the rumors I've been hearing. The others... they put up with him for everything he did for the A'ras, but they all say that he's slipping. Much longer, and I think the other masters will send him off."

She wouldn't argue with Samis, but it troubled her that rumors were spreading about Invar losing his mind. Carth hadn't seen anything that would make her think that his mind had gone. He was still sharp.

"Be careful, Rel. I think it's good that you've been raised to sai, but now that you're out of the palace grounds, it gets more dangerous. And it's been getting more and more dangerous over the last few weeks. I... I don't want anything to happen to you."

She shook her head. "Nothing will."

Samis flashed that disarming smile of his. "Good. Now,

I'm supposed to report back to Erik. I don't know what they have planned for tonight, but I'd better not keep them waiting."

When he left her, Carth stood in the growing night, watching him depart. In spite of the attacks, she felt strangely hopeful. She'd been raised to sai. Trista and Devn seemed to have warmed to her. Alison was back as her friend. And Samis… there was something there, even if she didn't know what it was.

With everything seeming to come together, why did she feel a growing discomfort?

Chapter 22

Carth was awakened by a hand on her shoulder, her heart pounding.

She sat up, reaching for the knife she kept beneath her pillow as she scanned her room. She strained for the shadows, but they didn't respond.

Samis grabbed her wrist and kept her from reaching her knife. "It's me, Rel."

"Samis? What are you doing here?"

"Come on. You're needed."

"For what?"

"I don't know. The other A'ras sent me to get you. They were going to send Landon, but I volunteered. Hope you don't mind."

"You're better than Landon," she said, sitting up and rubbing the sleep from her eyes. Samis pulled his hand off her wrist, and she grabbed her knife. Carth got up and dressed quickly, appreciative of the fact that Samis had turned away. She'd been dressed—one of the lessons the ashai learned was that you had to be prepared for awakening at any time of day—but not fully, wearing nothing more than a nearly sheer slip.

As soon as she was dressed, she stuffed her knife into the sheath on her waist. "What can you tell me?"

They started out of the cosak, and Carth noted the other sai coming from their rooms as well. Not only she had been roused, it seemed. There were nearly a dozen sai, each partnered with two A'ras to make a patrol, so for all of them to be dragged out of bed in the middle of the night meant something was happening.

Carth waited, partly expecting the rolling nausea to hit, but it never came. Not Hjan, then.

"There's not much I can tell you, mostly because I don't know myself. I got woken and told to get others."

They hurried across the yard, moving quietly in the night. She took a moment to try and detect anything else that might explain why she'd been woken, but found nothing.

It had been days since the Reshian attack, days that had passed quickly. Patrols had been benign, and Carth's connection with Trista and Devn had continued to improve. Now they no longer ignored her as they patrolled, even included her in conversations discussing where they would patrol next. They hadn't encountered any more of the Reshian, but she sensed that neither of them wanted to encounter any further threats. The last one had shaken them, and through the conversations she'd overheard, part of that fear came from the fact that they recognized that they wouldn't have fared quite as well had Carth not been there.

In some ways, that created a different sort of isolation.

They reached the gate and found a collection of A'ras waiting. Trista and Devn were among them, and both nodded to her. Samis left her with them without saying another word.

"What is this?" Carth asked.

"Another attack," Devn said.

"Reshian?"

Trista nodded. Her eyes were bloodshot and she carried the stench of ale. Was she safe to be out here? "We think so, Rel. Don't know much more than what we've been told, and that isn't too much, either."

"Why so many?"

Trista glanced at Devn before answering. "A team was killed, Rel. All of them."

Carth's breath caught.

"I know you've been in other situations, so we're not worried about you, but... we need to be safe. Use your potential, and be ready."

"For what?"

Trista shook her head. "For anything."

They started through the gate, partnered up with another team. Carth didn't know the A'ras on the team, but the sai was an older girl named Leah. She nodded to Carth but didn't say anything more.

Trista led the patrol. Rather than the spiral she usually used as they left the palace grounds, one that Carth had discovered helped ensure that they covered as much ground as possible, she marched them quickly through the streets, and they made their way toward the docks.

Carth kept her eyes focused straight in front but wrapped the shadows around her, ready for whatever attack they might encounter. She didn't even bother holding on to the A'ras magic. At night, she could use the shadows more effectively anyway. Besides that, she worried that if the Reshian used the shadows, she would need to be ready.

Few people were out in the streets, but when they saw the A'ras, they went running, scattering. It left the streets with an ominous and empty feeling, one that Carth had never experienced in her time living along the docks. There were always people out.

As they neared the docks, she felt a flash of pressure against the shadows. Someone moved through them, someone who was aware of the shadows and knew how to use them.

"There's something up there," Carth said.

Trista looked back at her. "You sure?"

She nodded. "Don't know what it is, but I can feel it."

Trista looked over at Devn. "Be ready."

"You're going by what Rel has to say?" one of the A'ras asked.

Trista turned sharply to the man. She was about a foot shorter and quite a bit lighter than he was, but she made him take a step back. "Damn right, I am. Rel kept us alive. Kept Master Invar alive. The least we can do is listen to her."

Trista tapped Carth on the arm. "Where now, Rel?"

Carth focused on her connection to the shadows, noting how whatever she sensed cut through her connection. It was a strange sensation, one that she wasn't even sure of the meaning of, but the sense of it was distinct, and real.

She pointed at the strongest surge.

Trista started in that direction.

They had reached the River Road, which appeared different than it normally did. Carth struggled to figure out what she detected before realizing that it came from shadows diffusing across the street, growing thicker, almost like a fog.

"Can't see anything down here," one of the other A'ras commented.

"Fog coming off the river," the other said.

They disappeared into the shadows, going off down the road, away from the thickest part obscuring the street, leaving Carth, Devn, and Trista alone.

"It's not fog, is it?" Devn said.

Carth could see him looking at her. Did he know she could use the shadows? Did he know that she could see through them as well?

"It's not fog," she said.

"You know what this is?" he asked, getting close enough that he could whisper.

"Shadows. The Reshian can use them."

Devn breathed out. "Should have known there was something more to them."

"You don't seem surprised," Carth said.

"There have been rumors of the Reshian possessing some sort of ability for a while. Didn't think it would be anything like this."

Carth felt movement near the shore. "They're near the warehouses," she said.

"How do you know?" Trista had gotten closer, and listened to them.

"Because I can use the shadows too."

"That's how you saved Invar, isn't it?"

"Yes."

"And the attack?"

She nodded.

"Good. We'll need whatever we can get to keep us safe. If you can use it, then you should be leading it."

Carth swallowed. They expected her to lead. She wasn't sure she was ready to lead, not when it came to the A'ras. It was one thing for her to go running off into the darkness on her own, with only herself to worry about, but it was much different when she was responsible for making sure that others were safe as well. She would have to make sure that Trista and Devn weren't injured. That would be on her, and if she somehow failed—if the shadows kept them from determining what was coming—that would be on Carth.

"Stay close to me," she said.

"Why?" Trista asked.

Carth pulled on the shadows, cloaking them. As she did, it created something of a shimmery light that parted the depths of the shadows, making it so that they could see easier.

"What happened?" Devn asked.

"I cloaked us."

"Cloak?"

"It's something I can do with the shadows. I can use them to pull around me. Us, I guess. We're able to use the shadows that way."

"Why does it seem like you made it brighter?"

"Because something of the shadows shifted, coming around us but releasing around the rest of the street. That's about as well as I understand it."

"How long have you been doing this?" Trista asked.

"Before I came to the palace, but since I've been there, I can't detect them the same way. Until recently."

"The attack?" Devn asked.

"The attack disrupted something along the wall, the barriers that restrict my access."

"But not in the street?"

"Not the rest of the city."

Trista glanced at Devn. "Good."

Carth moved quickly forward, staring through the darkness. The sense of someone pushing through the shadows persisted, but she couldn't tell where they were. Veering toward shore, she waited, focusing on the sense of pressure. Creeping along the shore, she held on to the shadows, letting them cling to her. Wrapped in them as she was, she didn't detect anything.

Would it matter if she added A'ras magic?

Gritting her teeth, she pulled on the sense of it deep within her, tearing it as it flowed through her. The magic came slowly, oozing toward her, and she grasped enough to add into the shadow blessing. It was only a trickle, barely anything, but as she did, the shadows shifted. There was no other way for her to describe it. The pressure she'd detected again was there, this time clearly only a few steps from her.

And not alone.

Nearly a dozen.

Too many for them to handle by themselves.

The attackers seemed to realize she'd noticed them. They moved quickly toward her.

What could she do? The shadows didn't help, not against people who had some ability with them. It was possible they couldn't use the shadows the same way she could, but even if they only shrouded themselves, that was enough to make it impossible for Trista and Devn, let alone the other A'ras patrol, to help.

Running wasn't an option. The river was a torrent behind them, the rapids giving the only noise in the otherwise muted night. The Reshian in front of them prevented them from getting past.

But they were A'ras. Carth might not be full A'ras—not yet—but she couldn't run, not while these men threatened the city.

There was one thing she hadn't tried, and she didn't know if it would work if she did.

"Be ready," she whispered to Trista and Devn.

Carth reached for the shadows and *pulled*.

Tearing the sense of the shadows away from the Reshian felt similar to trying to pull the A'ras magic from herself. It came slowly, almost painfully, oozing away. Had she not had the experience with that magic, and had she not practiced fighting through it, she would have given up.

Carth screamed.

They were nearly upon her.

Taking a deep breath, she pulled one more time.

The shadows parted, leaving natural night.

Carth released them, pushing them across the river.

Trista and Devn leaped past her, attacking in an onslaught of activity.

Carth stood, unable to move for a moment. When the first attack came at her, she moved slowly, as if dazed, and managed to block the sword swinging toward her. The second would hit her. She saw it but couldn't do anything to stop it.

Another was there, the sword catching the one meant for her and turning the blade.

Carth took a step back and stumbled.

Samis.

"Get up, Rel. I think we'll need your help for this one."

She took a breath and stood. Magic flared around her, burning through her skin from all the A'ras attacking. Carth joined in, her strength gradually returning. She helped Samis with the man he faced, then moved on to another, trying to grab for the A'ras magic as she did but failing. The next came at her more quickly than she could react and she pulled on the shadows, sending them through the knife as she did. His eyes widened as he died.

Then it was done.

Carth wandered through the fallen, staring at each face, trying to understand what had happened. Nearly a hundred Reshian were here, and all had died. Blood was everywhere, leaving the street covered. Carth wanted nothing more than for the river to rise up and wash it away.

There were downed A'ras as well, caught by superior

numbers. She studied the faces, recognizing some, fearful that she'd find Samis.

Trista.

The woman stared up blankly, stabbed through the heart. Carth swallowed back a lump in her throat. Near her, she found Devn, still breathing, but with the wound in his side, he wouldn't be for long.

Carth crouched next to him and took his hand. "Devn," she whispered.

"Did good, Rel," he whispered.

"I wish I could've—"

He tried raising his hand but couldn't. "You did good. Shouldn't have been so many. Not sure how... not sure how..." He never finished.

Carth remained by him, unable to move.

Devn and Trista hadn't been her friends. They had barely welcomed her to their patrol, but they shouldn't have died. Not like this, not against the shadows.

Why?

Why would the Reshian attack like this?

She felt a hand on her shoulder and spun.

Samis stood behind her, his sword dipping toward the ground. Blood spattered his face and clothes. His eyes were wide and haunted.

"Rel?" he said. "This is your shadow magic?"

Carth didn't know what to say to him. How did she answer that the Reshian had used the shadows? How could she convince him that she was nothing like them? If she did, would he believe her? Would he ever see her the same way?

When she stood and sheathed her knife, she started to turn away, unable to answer. Afraid to answer.

Samis caught her wrist, pulled her toward him, and hugged her.

Chapter 23

The palace yard felt empty, matching the hollowness inside Carth.

Nearly fifty A'ras and sai had died, their bodies brought back to the palace and prepared for the funeral pyre. A somber air hung about the grounds, and no one really spoke. The classes for the ashai went on, but many of the instructors were gone, never to return. Of the dozen or so sai, only a few remained. Samis. Landon. Brita. Herself. That was it.

Carth no longer had a patrol and found herself wandering the grounds aimlessly. Most of the patrols had been disbanded, kept within the palace grounds with A'ras stationed along the top of the walls only, leaving the gates closed. She had no assignment, leaving her to wander. It wouldn't be a problem if there had been anyone for her to talk to, but so many had died, and those who remained living were in nearly as much shock as she was.

Fortifications along the wall had an urgency to them. The masters and remaining A'ras worked together, leaving a constant burning sensation through her as they used their magic. It might stop the Reshian, but it would do nothing to stop the Hjan. Carth suspected they worked together.

Alison gave her space, and for that, Carth was grateful. But Samis also gave her space, and she would have liked having him to speak to. It left her with an emptiness.

More than once, she'd tried going to the palace to find Invar, but each time, either he was gone or the masters were unavailable. Carth couldn't even be angry. There had been so many lost that she knew her struggles were minor compared to what others were going through.

In some ways, she felt as trapped as she had ever felt. She might be able to get past the walls, and she might be able to wander the city streets, but she didn't want to. Not when there were others who could use the shadows, others with a similar ability as hers, only they were intent on destroying the A'ras.

After the Reshian attack, no one spoke about the possibility of another Hjan attack. The last one had been weeks ago now, and Invar claimed there had been something placed that would protect the city, but that didn't make Carth any more comfortable with the prospect of what might be coming.

Late in the third day after the Reshian Massacre—as it was now called—she stood along the wall, running her hands through the ivy, wanting nothing more than for things to be as simple as they had been only a few months before. She might have been trapped on the palace grounds, but she'd been safe. There hadn't been the attacks on the city. There hadn't been a massacre of people she knew.

She reached a place where shadows coalesced and she stretched for them without thinking, pulling them toward her. The wall didn't prevent her from reaching them as it had. Carth held on to the shadows, letting them swirl around her, before releasing them again.

"Do you have to do that?"

Carth turned. Samis stood next to the wall, far enough out that he was no longer in the shadows. "I wasn't doing anything."

"I saw what you did. That's what happened that night, wasn't it? They use the shadows, same as you."

"They don't use them the same as me."

"Maybe not the same, but similar."

Carth traced her hand along the ivy. "I don't know that they could even use the shadows. They cloaked themselves, but it was different."

Samis watched her, and she noted that his eyes were slightly reddened. His hand hovered over the hilt of his sword, as if he were ready to unsheathe it at any moment. "Are they the same as you?"

Carth flushed with anger. "Have I ever attacked the A'ras?"

Samis blinked and shook his head. "I'm... I'm sorry, Carth. It's just that this attack..."

The night of the massacre, they'd shared a moment, but that felt like so long ago now. She didn't know how Samis saw her, but the fact that he asked about whether she was like the Reshian made her angry.

"I know what happened with the attack. Had I not pulled

the shadows away, it would have been worse."

"I know that."

"Then don't come here accusing me of being anything like them!"

Samis let out a long sigh. "I don't know what to do. I've trained to become A'ras, raised to sai, and thought that made me unstoppable." He fell silent for a moment. "Do you know the Aren intend a testing?"

"I haven't heard from anyone since the attack," she said. "My patrol was destroyed."

Samis dropped his hands to his sides. "Mine too. That's why I... I'm sorry, Rel."

"For what?"

He rubbed his eyes again and turned away from her. Carth felt a surge of power and realized that it came from all around her. It came on suddenly, and in a rush, making her skin and mouth dry. As she looked around to see where it came from, she noted three masters approaching.

None were Invar.

"Samis?" she said.

He continued away from her.

Carth knew what had happened then. Samis had told the masters about her ability with the shadows. The others who might know—Trista and Devn—were both killed. Invar knew but had never seemed all that concerned, but that had been before the Reshian attack.

"Ms. Rel," Master Harrison said as he neared.

She turned toward them.

"You will accompany us."

She looked to Lyanna, to Master Erind, and then to Master Harrison. "What did I do?"

"You admit that you did something?"

"I didn't—"

Lyanna and Erind grabbed her arms. As they did, Carth noted the surge of magic through them and felt how it tamped out the connection to the shadows.

"What are you doing?" she asked.

"You will come with us. We have questions for you," Harrison said.

"Where's Master Invar?"

Lyanna gave a questioning look to Harrison, but he ignored it. "Invar has been relieved as master."

Carth tried looking back at Samis and found him standing along the wall, watching her with his reddened eyes. When she caught his gaze, he looked down, unable to meet her eyes.

The masters dragged her along the palace lawn. At first she thought they might bring her to the palace, but they didn't. Instead, they took her to the small, squat building behind the palace, one the ashai all assumed was meant for storage, though none had ever seen anyone go inside. With a surge of power, Harrison pulled the door open. Stairs led into the earth, descending quickly into darkness. Lyanna and Erind pulled her with them. Carth didn't even argue. Lanterns blazed on the wall, and it took Carth a moment to note that they had power coursing through them. Not ordinary light, but magically infused so that it pushed back the shadows. In some ways, it reminded her of what the

Hjan had used to heal themselves from her shadows.

They placed her into an empty room. Harrison made a path around the perimeter of the room, layering a barrier of magic as he did. With each layer, Carth's ability to reach the shadows faded, eventually disappearing altogether. She tried reaching for A'ras magic and found that impossible as well.

Lyanna and Erind released her and stepped across the barrier that Harrison had created. The three of them used another surge of power—Carth could still feel the effect of the magic even if she couldn't reach it.

"Why are you doing this to me?" she asked.

"We have questioned many in the aftermath of the massacre," Harrison said.

"You never questioned *me.*"

"There is no need. Those who were there saw what you did, and all commented on the way you used a dark attack."

"I didn't use the darkness to attack!"

Harrison came closer to the barrier he had placed but didn't cross over it. "How long have you worked with the Reshian?"

Carth blinked. This couldn't be happening. They couldn't believe that she would actually *work* with the Reshian, could they? "I'm not with them. I've been here... studying as A'ras."

"You came late for our students. I should have questioned more when you first came, but Avera vouched for you."

"Then get Avera!"

"Unfortunately, she is gone."

"Master Invar knows me. He's been working with me!"

"Invar. That man has grown foolish in the last few years, always worried about a different threat, ignoring the real threat we've struggled against for the last two years. Tell me, Ms. Rel, how did you convince Invar to help you? Did you seduce him?"

Carth couldn't even answer. The idea shocked her, but everything else they accused her of doing shocked her just as much. This couldn't be happening to her. It felt unreal... but here she was, separated from the shadows, separated from everyone she knew and cared about, treated like she was nothing more than a criminal.

"Where is he?" she asked.

Harrison stepped back and started to leave.

"Why are you doing this?"

Harrison paused. "You're a danger, Rel. You and the Reshian. You've brought destruction into the city, and now we must find a way to restore peace."

Harrison left her, Lyanna and Erind following.

Carth ran after them, but the barrier Harrison had placed pushed her back. She screamed as she struck it, feeling as if her skin were seared, then tried again. Each time, she failed.

She was trapped.

Chapter 24

Carth lost track of time.

Her body ached from repeated attempts to cross the barrier, each time leaving her no closer than she'd been before, each time leaving her skin feeling as if it might peel off. Her head throbbed, a steady aching sensation that left her vision blurred at times. Worse, she needed sleep, but each time she tried, she jerked awake, feeling like there was someone watching her.

Nothing made sense. Why would the masters blame her for working with the Reshian? She'd *helped* the A'ras, hadn't she?

But the Reshian could use the shadows, just like she could.

Only, she couldn't reach the shadows here and hadn't managed to reach the shadows most of the time she'd been within the yard. Only after the initial attack had she managed to reach them again.

Why could the A'ras withhold the shadows but not keep the Hjan from attacking? Why had the A'ras mastered withholding the shadows but not repelling the other kind of attack?

Those were the kind of thoughts that plagued her.

Occasionally, others would come, but mostly to bring food. That was it. Carth had two meals, with water added to them, but the A'ras assigned to bring her food never spoke to her.

She lost track of time. Lanterns burned brightly in the room and the walls were a white stone, almost as if everything was meant to defeat the shadows.

When a door opened above her, she thought it might be time for another meal, but the last had not been all that long ago. How could it be time for another?

Soft footsteps came down the stairs. Carth turned toward her captor, expecting another one of the A'ras. It was Harrison.

"Master Harrison?" she asked.

He stood on the other side of the barrier, his hands clasped behind his back. He appeared thinner than she remembered, his face almost ruddy, and the skin sagged on his cheeks. "Ms. Rel. I admit I am sorry that it came to this. We thought we could help you before it did."

Hope that Harrison might have come to release her faded as he stood on the other side of the barrier. He remained there, as if perfectly aware of how far he could step before he reached the edge and did not want to cross beyond that.

"Why? What are you talking about?"

"You are Ih-lash."

Carth's breath caught. "You knew?"

"I didn't know, but Invar... that fool thought to help you while know that the Reshian were descended of the Ih-lash."

Carth's heart flipped. "Invar?"

"Invar knew the challenge."

"Why didn't he tell me?"

"We wanted to know if you were with them. He doubted that you were. Invar thought your story was too traumatic, one that he didn't think you would be able to fabricate, but it was possible. That was the reason he sent you on patrol."

She closed her eyes. "Not because I deserved to be elevated." Could Invar really have lied to her about that? He'd led her to believe that she *could* be one of the A'ras after so much time spent doubting herself. Because of Invar, she had almost allowed herself to imagine finally becoming one of the A'ras. She was the one who had been the fool.

"It is possible that you have the necessary talent, Ms. Rel. Invar could not have gotten away with it if you did not, but I suspect you have other ways of demonstrating your ability, don't you?"

"Why would I do that?"

Harrison paced along the edge of the barrier. "The Reshian have grown bolder the last few years. They haven't pressed into the city—the patrols served to keep them back—but they have attacked the A'ras caravans outside the city. I thought it possible that you might know where to find them."

"I'm not with the Reshian," Carth said.

"When you noted the first attack, we still didn't know.

You have never been able to reach the A'ras flame nearly as easily as others, but there was no questioning the fact that you did, in fact, reach it. That is the reason you were permitted to remain."

"Harrison—"

"And then the Hjan attacked. Invar reported that you led him to them and claimed to fight them off. That wasn't even Hjan, I suspect, but Reshian."

"I *did* fight off the Hjan."

"Perhaps. Trista claimed that you helped her and Devn in the streets, but again, that was against the Reshian. You see the challenge, don't you, Ms. Rel?"

"I don't see anything."

"Hmm. If you work with the Reshian, you would say that, wouldn't you? The Reshian have grown too powerful lately, and now, after the massacre... well, we are not strong enough to withstand another attack. If we fall, the entire northland falls, and the A'ras will not be responsible for that. We know what the Reshian want, and we know that they are powerful enough to overwhelm fully trained A'ras, which is why we have sought an alliance. In exchange for peace, they asked only one thing."

Carth couldn't think of what allies he might mean. Would it be men like Jhon? He had some abilities, though she hadn't determined what those were. Or was there something else?

"What did they ask for?"

"You." He turned to the stairs and paused. "In some ways, Ms. Rel, I am sorry, but then I remember what you have done to us."

"Who? Who wants me?"

"I do not know what they want of you, but if it prevents additional attacks and pits them against the Reshian, the price is worth it."

"Who do you mean?"

"It doesn't matter to you anymore. They will take care of the Reshian threat. They have proven they are capable of it. That is enough."

"The *Hjan*? That's who you mean?"

"Goodbye, Ms. Rel."

He started up the stairs, leaving her trapped in the room.

The masters had made an agreement with the Hjan. And they had agreed to trade Carth for perceived safety.

"There is no bargaining when it comes to the Hjan!" she shouted after him.

The door opened and then closed, leaving her alone. Carth paced around the inside of the barrier. She needed to reach the shadows, or the A'ras magic, anything that would help her find a way to get free. She didn't have to be stronger than the barrier Master Harrison placed, only find a way to disrupt it, much like the Hjan had disrupted the barrier around the wall. A barrier she now knew was intended to hold back the Reshian.

She attempted to throw herself at the barrier but had the same experience she had before. Pain surged through her, but terror gave her renewed focus. She did it again, and again, but the outcome was no different.

She sagged to the ground.

If she couldn't get free, eventually the Hjan would come

for her. When her stomach flipped and the nausea came, she'd know her time was up.

When it came, she still wasn't prepared.

Waves of nausea hit.

They came over and over. Carth imagined the flickering as the Hjan appeared.

Her breathing quickened. Were the masters—was Harrison—giving the Hjan access to the inside of the palace grounds? After the attacks they had already suffered, how could he do that?

A door opened. Carth noticed it as a stirring of the air, a gentle fluttering that told her she would no longer be alone. She wanted to stand, but it didn't matter. Not now.

"Get up, Ms. Rel."

She looked up and saw Invar standing on the edge of the barrier, wearing a pained expression. "Why? You want to bring me to the Hjan?"

His thin face darkened, making him appear even older. "Because you may be the only one who will be able to help us."

"Harrison said—"

"Harrison is a fool. He remains stuck in the past, not able to move beyond old anger. That comes from his heritage and connection to the Alisant family. There are others like him who continue ancient hatred, unable to see beyond the past. Now, do you intend to get moving or will you remain here until they come for you?"

"I'm not with the Reshian."

"I know you're not, Ms. Rel, much as I know that you saved

232

me from the Hjan attack. Twice. It *was* Hjan, regardless of what Harrison has managed to convince Lyanna and Erind."

"Harrison said you suspected that I was with the Reshian."

"He knows nothing, Ms. Rel."

"He's one of the masters…"

"Tell me, do you feel magic working now?"

She frowned but nodded. She could point out where the magic flowed around her, creating the barrier, as well as the magic that Invar used to disrupt it. "Yes."

"There are probably five people on these grounds able to detect the power of the flame, Ms. Rel."

"Who else? You?"

He nodded. "Most who study here can only reach an echo of the flame. They can reach it when it burns here, but they have no deeper connection. That flame has burned here for centuries, brought here by the A'ras ancestors, and it is the reason the palace has remained protected. It is the reason the first family chose Nyaesh as the seat of their power. Now is not the time for a history lesson, but know that most only reach the reflection of a greater power."

"I don't understand."

He smiled at her. "There are very few with the ability to reach the true flame, Ms. Rel. Not in many years. If we survive this, you will learn why."

"What is the flame?" she asked.

"It is something that reveals itself in unique ways. Some manage incredible strength. Some have visions. Others develop sensitivity to it."

"Me?"

He smiled sadly. "Yes, Ms. Rel. You have an ability to reach the flame. Not the reflection, but the true flame. That, I suspect, is why it is so difficult for you to access it, but also why, when you do, you manage such strength."

"Why does any of that matter?"

"It does not, other than for me to tell you that I believe you. I have waited for years for another with the ability to reach the flame. That is why I chose you." He stepped across the barrier and held his hand out toward her. "Now, come with me, Ms. Rel. It is time for you to leave."

"Leave?"

"This cell. Come."

Carth reached for his hand and stood. He led her across the barrier, and a painful searing raced through her before disappearing as she crossed.

On the other side, the sense of both shadows and A'ras magic—the flame—returned. She wrapped herself in the shadows and sent them through her knife.

"This should never have been done to you," Invar said softly.

They hurried up the steps. Another wave of nausea struck her. Carth shivered and nearly fell forward, struggling under the pain.

"Fight this, Ms. Rel. It will pass."

"How do you know?"

"I don't, but I need for it to pass. Otherwise, the A'ras will fall, which means Nyaesh will fall. We have stood for countless generations and cannot fail now."

They emerged into the space above and Invar pushed open the door.

He pulled on a surge of profound power, more than she had ever detected from him before, enough that there was no question that he drew upon more than what most of the other A'ras reached.

On the other side of the door, she saw over a dozen of the Hjan as they flickered across the palace grounds. All seemed to be heading toward the palace.

"What do they want?" she wondered, but she didn't expect an answer.

"The fool," he whispered.

"What?"

"Me. I thought they wanted access to the Alisant, but that isn't it at all."

"What then?"

"Can you feel it? They would extinguish the flame. They would leave the north helpless. We cannot let that happen, Ms. Rel." He unsheathed a pair of curved blades with handles almost more decorative than functional, and then slipped both her father's knife and the one he'd made her out of a hidden pocket, handing them to her. "Are you ready to fight?"

Carth thought about *why* she would be fighting. The A'ras masters wouldn't want her fighting, so why should she? "What if I don't?"

"If you don't, then Nyaesh will fall, much like Ih-lash. Others as well. The A'ras are but one barrier, but an important one, Ms. Rel."

She frowned as she studied him, realizing something. "Are you even A'ras?"

Invar winked. "Jhon told me that you had a quick mind. I am A'ras, but I would be a part of something else as well if they would have me."

Jhon. She hadn't seen him—or heard from him—since he'd sent her to the A'ras. He must have known that Invar would be here, and that she would have someone who would teach her, even if he had never seemed particularly inclined before now.

"What else? Why did he send me here?"

"That is an answer that you deserve, but one that will only come if we survive. Know for now that it was your mother's will for you to come here. Now, Ms. Rel, unsheathe your knives and use both the shadow and the flame."

Chapter 25

Carth slipped from the building, shadows swirling around her.

Invar followed her, power burning from him with such amazing magnitude.

Carth didn't have a chance to focus on it. A pair of Hjan flickered in front of her.

She sliced with her knife, catching the first man with the end of her blade and pushing shadows into him. They poured out, filling him. She remembered how the other Hjan had used some sort of light magic to defeat the shadows, so Carth forced more and more into him.

"That will be plenty," Invar said.

She jerked around and saw the other Hjan lying on the ground. "I thought you couldn't defeat the Hjan."

"You're not the only one who can learn, Ms. Rel."

"That's where you've been?"

"When I realized the depths of the threat, I knew that I had to find out all I could. It was inevitable that they would attack again."

"Where are we going?" Carth asked.

"The palace. That is where the flame has been since the founding of Nyaesh."

"And what happens if they extinguish it?"

Another Hjan appeared, and Invar slipped forward so quickly that he was a blur, striking the Hjan in the chest and sending a surge of A'ras power through him. Maybe it was not A'ras power, but the flame.

"As I have said, if they extinguish the flame, we will be in danger. Not you and I, but the people of the north. It is one layer of protection against those with power in the south."

"It burned me," she admitted, holding her hand out to him.

"You can reach the flame, Ms. Rel. You were never in any real danger from it."

He motioned for her to follow, and they reached the palace.

The doors hung open, one in splinters. A body lay at an odd angle on the other side of the door. The spray of blond hair was familiar.

"Lyanna?" Invar whispered. He shook his head. "Damn you, Harrison. What were you thinking?"

His knives seemed to flow, as if the metal were liquid, and he stepped into the hall. A rolling sense of nausea struck her, and five Hjan appeared.

"Ms. Rel, I think that we will need all of your abilities now," Invar managed to say more calmly.

Carth took a deep breath. The Hjan had attacked her parents. They had killed her mother, likely her father. And now they wanted to take the A'ras and the safety of the north. The A'ras might have abandoned her, but she would not abandon them.

Shadows swirled around her. Carth drew on them.

To this, she added the touch of her A'ras magic.

It burned.

And then ignited power.

Everything slowed.

She streaked forward, slicing as she did, catching each of the Hjan in the blink of an eye. She stopped next to Invar and pushed the shadows into them, using the combined effects of her power.

Time surged forward again.

The Hjan seemed to stutter as they tried to flicker, but failed.

They fell, almost as one.

Carth waited, pushing more shadows into them.

The man nearest her rolled toward her and flicked something toward her.

Invar dove and caught it with his knife, flipping it back to the Hjan. They stopped moving, stopped breathing.

Invar raced along the corridor to Master Hall. The door was open. On the other side, Erind lay unmoving. Harrison sat slumped along the wall, his eyes glossy. He looked up as they entered and his mouth moved, but he didn't say anything.

Several of the Hjan flickered.

Carth again reached for shadows and flame, drawing them toward her. Power filled her, but the Hjan seemed ready for it this time. Unlike before, there was no stalling of time. They slashed toward her.

Carth ducked and sliced up with the knives. She twisted the one that might have been her father's as well as the one that Invar had given her.

The nearest fell as Invar cut him down. Carth pressed shadows through her and caught the next two with her knives, hitting them with shadows.

Invar caught two more using a powerful draw of magic.

That left only one.

She'd seen him before. It was the man who had attacked Invar in the street.

He grinned when he saw her. "Not shadow blessed at all, are you? You are shadow born. We have yet to study one of the shadow born. I think that when we take you—"

Blood bloomed across his chest.

Harrison crouched behind him, his sword held between his hands. He sagged to the ground without saying anything more, the Hjan falling on top of him.

Carth shivered and looked around the Master Hall. The huge fire that had been here when she'd last come was gone, extinguished. The flame they had come to protect was gone. They were too late.

Invar touched the metal of the basin that had once held the fire. "All these years it has served as a barrier, as a marker, and now... now it is gone." He turned to Harrison, anger flashing in his eyes. "You were a fool, Harrison, but you did not deserve this."

"What can we do?"

"The fight out there will be up to you, Ms. Rel."

"I can't—"

"Ah, Ms. Rel, the Hjan were correct when it came to you. You are not shadow blessed, but shadow born."

"I don't understand."

"It is why you can use the shadows the way you can. Shadow born are rarer than those with the ability to reach the flame, and more dangerous. I understand why they would want to study you, but you cannot let them succeed. You must fight, Ms. Rel. We must expel the Hjan from the grounds."

She looked at the men fallen in front of her. How much more could she do? How much would she be responsible for? "If I do this, what will you do?"

"The flame, Ms. Rel. It must be relit."

"Can you do that?"

Invar stared at it. "I must. And now you must go."

Carth took one more look around the Master Hall, then rushed out of the palace. She encountered no other Hjan as she did and found no A'ras, either. The halls were empty, holding only the bodies.

Outside was different.

Flickers sent nausea rolling through her. There was a direction to it. The cosak.

It hadn't been enough for the Hjan to extinguish the flame and kill the masters, but they had to go after the ashai?

Alison was there.

Samis, too. Did she care enough about Samis after what he'd done?

As she ran across the grounds, she realized that she did. She couldn't let him get killed for stupidity.

A flicker appeared in front of her, and Carth, wrapped with shadows and flame, stabbed the Hjan that appeared. She didn't wait to see if he would get back up. She raced forward and saw the cosak coming into view. The sounds of scattered screams reached her.

Her stomach rolled, but not because of the Hjan.

This had been her home for the last few years. These were people she knew.

A pair of Hjan flickered into view in front of her.

Carth lunged, reaching away with both of her knives, sending shadows into her father's knife and flame through the one Invar had given her.

She twisted, and the attacker slapped her knives out of her hands.

The Hjan nearest her smirked.

Carth reached for the shadows, cloaking herself with them.

As she did, she kicked, rolling toward her fallen knife. She managed to reach it and twisted, slicing as she did toward the nearest Hjan. She caught him on the arm, and he fell. Light surged from a knife, much like it had when the one Hjan had somehow reversed the effect of her shadows. Carth kicked at his hand, and the knife went flying. She sent the shadows through him, flooding him with darkness. He convulsed and stopped moving.

The other Hjan had escaped in the attack. Carth ran toward the cosak. Much like at the palace, the doors were open. She saw a small form lying unmoving on the other side of the door. Carth didn't want to check, but she had to know. She rolled the body over. Elian. He was new to the A'ras and often had a sharp tongue, but no one deserved this.

Nausea struck her, and she looked up.

A Hjan at the end of the hall noticed her crouching there. "We had cleared this place," he said. "Come with us, girl, if you wish to survive."

"Come with you?" She couldn't think of anything else to say.

"You would have to be sensitive to be here. You will be given the opportunity to join, and if you choose otherwise..."

Was that the reason the Hjan had come to the palace? Had they intended to abduct children, making this no different than what she'd stopped near the docks years ago?

The Hjan stalked toward her, flickering as he came.

Carth didn't move. She needed to know what they intended. If the Hjan were taking the ashai, then she would need to help them.

As he neared, he seemed to realize that she wasn't as concerned as she should have been. He flickered, reappearing behind her.

Carth spun, pulling on shadows as she did.

They swirled around her, and she sliced at the Hjan, her first attack missing. His didn't.

When his blade cut her arm, Carth screamed and nearly lost her knife.

Pain burned through her, but with a strange sensation,

one that felt almost like her magic seeped out. Could the Hjan somehow steal her magic, siphoning it off?

She jumped back and pulled on the shadows, but the connection was different now. Weaker.

The Hjan smiled, as if he knew what effect his blade would have on her flesh, and flickered toward her.

Carth knew she should run. If she was injured and lost control of her magic, the only advantage she possessed would be gone.

Behind her, she caught sight of Alison leading a pair of younger students through the hall. Her eyes widened when she noticed Carth.

Carth tore at the shadows, tore at the magic burning within her, the flame of the A'ras, and let that power fill her. It flowed out of her and she drew it back, demanding that it assist her with the attack.

The pain in her arm eased.

The Hjan tried to flicker again, but she used a swirling of shadows and held him. He couldn't move.

"Where are they?" she demanded.

The Hjan only smiled. "You're too late, shadow born. There's nothing you can do to save the others. We have won. The rest of the north will be ours."

Carth stabbed her knife into his stomach and twisted. "Not while I live."

Darkness flooded into him and he slipped to the ground. He tried to flicker, but failed.

Alison started toward her before stopping.

Her sudden halt forced Carth to spin.

Three Hjan had appeared behind her.

There were too many. She struggled to keep up, but the rest of the A'ras would not be able to help. It *had* to be her.

Worse, for the first time, she began to feel fatigued when using the shadows. How much longer would she even be able to keep up the fight?

Someone behind her cried out.

Carth hazarded a glance. Another two Hjan were behind her.

Too many.

Had Invar been with her, he might have been able to help, but he had remained in the Master Hall to relight the flame.

Carth took a deep breath.

She would fall here. The Hjan would kill her, finally finish off the family they had tried to destroy all those years before, but she would do as much damage as possible before they did.

Shadow and darkness flowed through her, along with the burning sense of the A'ras magic. Carth drew all of that in, letting it power her through this final attack. If nothing else, she would save her friend.

She released the power she held.

Time stood still for a moment.

It was the briefest span, short enough that she wasn't sure it was real, but long enough that she had the advantage, and she sliced forward with her knives. Two of the Hjan fell before they could react.

Time surged forward.

She battled with the remaining Hjan, but she knew she was too slow. She could face one, even two when her magic was strong, but more than that would only get her killed.

She managed to stop the Hjan and spun around to find Alison fighting two Hjan next to Samis. Both appeared outmatched, but they did all they could to keep the Hjan from reaching her.

With another pull of power, she reached them and stabbed both Hjan as they began to turn.

Her power faded and she fell.

Had she done enough?

Nausea rolled within her. It meant more flickering and more Hjan.

Not enough. And now she didn't have the strength to do anything. Now her friends would die as well.

Chapter 26

Carth expected another attack, or more flickering, but there was none. No additional nausea rolled through her. No more Hjan appeared. It was almost as if they had finally disappeared. She didn't want to believe that and started to get up, but she was too weak. Exhaustion rolled through her, leaving her incapacitated.

Alison reached a hand for her, clasping her wrist and helping her up. "I don't know what that was," she started, "but no one can question your ability anymore, Carthenne Rel."

Carth tried to smile, but the sight of the dead bodies all around her made it so that she didn't *want* to smile. What she wanted was to lie down, let sleep claim her. Right now, she wouldn't even care if she ever woke up.

"What happened to you?" Alison asked. "Master Harrison claimed that you worked with the Reshian."

"I stopped the Reshian," she said. She wondered if even that had been a mistake. They were able to use the shadows, much like she could. They would have something they could teach her, lessons she began to realize that she needed, and that she wouldn't find if she remained here. "I've not been with them, regardless of what Harrison said."

"How did you get out?" Alison asked.

"Invar came for me when the attack started. He said I might be the only one who would really be able to help stop it."

She needed to get to Invar. If there was anything she could do to help, she needed to try. As tired as she was, it would have to wait until after everything else had been resolved.

Carth started toward the door, staggering as she did. Alison caught her, lifting her under the arms. Carth tried to shake her off, but couldn't. Alison held on.

"Let me help you," Alison said. "You've done enough for everyone. It's our turn to help you."

She started down the hall, and Carth could tell that Alison led her toward her room. She thought about letting Alison leave her there, but she couldn't do that yet. As much as she wanted to go to her room, she needed to learn what else had happened here.

"The palace," she said to Alison.

Alison shook her head. "It's not safe out there. It's probably not safe in here, either."

"I need to get back to Invar," she said.

"You always want to go *toward* trouble, don't you?"

Alison helped her from the cosak. Out in the yard, a battle was taking place, but not between the Hjan and the A'ras. Shadows swirled, shifting and moving, and Carth realized that the Reshian had attacked.

Alison gasped. "I thought you stopped the rest of them."

Carth blinked, and her mind felt thick. "I stopped the Hjan."

"There were no Hjan, Carth. Those were Reshian."

Enough strength had returned for Carth to stand unsupported. Staring through the shadows, she realized that the Reshian fought the remaining Hjan. "They weren't Reshian. *Those* are. And they're not attacking the A'ras," she said.

"It's the Reshian, Carth. You know what they did."

Carth had *thought* she knew what they did, but now she wasn't certain. The Reshian she saw fighting here made no effort to attack the A'ras who staggered through the yard. They kept their focus on the Hjan, targeting them only.

As she watched, the remaining A'ras began to organize. Landon was among them, as was Samis. They started toward the Reshian, swords drawn and a hint of magic burning, though not with the same strength they had only hours earlier.

"No!" Carth shouted.

Alison looked at her as if she had lost her mind. "Carth?"

Carth shrugged her off and hurried toward the A'ras. She might not have much strength, but she wasn't about to let the A'ras attack the Reshian, not when she suspected they had only been in the city because of the Hjan. They hadn't come to attack the A'ras... why would they when the A'ras served to protect the northlands? They were here because of the Hjan.

Alison tried grabbing at her arm, but Carth shook her off. She pulled on shadows, straining for the connection, and found that outside, in the fading light of day, the shadows came to her more easily. The A'ras flame burned softly within her as well, and she dragged on this sense. Using the two together, she wrapped shadows and magic around the collected A'ras, spinning it into an ever thicker band. It created a barrier, much like what Harrison had used to hold her in the cell, but this one, she created to prevent the A'ras from attacking.

"What did you do?" Alison asked. "I believed you! I thought you were with us!"

"I *am* with you."

"Then let the A'ras free. The Reshian—"

"Are not the enemy," Carth said. "Look!"

She pointed to a dozen shadow blessed who commanded the shadows, congealing them around a dozen or so Hjan. Reshian attacked Hjan, using a combination of shadows that swirled around the Hjan and prevented them from flickering. The Hjan were skilled, though, and disrupted the shadows, pushing back the Reshian.

The Hjan pressed the attack, and the Reshian faded back. Carth knew what needed to be done, though she didn't know if she had the strength to do it. It meant confirming the fears the A'ras had about her. It meant abandoning her friend Alison, abandoning the hope she had for anything more with this life, the one her parents had wanted for her. But if she didn't, the A'ras would suffer. Those she cared about would suffer. Wasn't that worth the sacrifice?

"I'm sorry, Alison."

She pushed Alison toward the other A'ras, holding her in the shadows and the flame.

The dawning horror and sadness on her face was hard to watch.

Carth couldn't watch. She turned to the Hjan, drawing on the shadows, feeling a surge of strength through her. The Reshian might be shadow blessed, but she was more than that. She knew that now. Not shadow cursed, not as she had begun to fear. She was connected to the shadows, could use them in some ways.

She was shadow born.

The Reshian seemed to recognize that she fought *with* them. They parted, letting her reach the Hjan. A face appeared among the Reshian and she nearly lost her focus.

Jhon?

He winked at her before disappearing again, caught in a swirl of shadows.

Carth attacked the Hjan using shadows and the flame. She moved faster than she thought possible with as weakened as she felt, attacking with a fury but no longer needing to fight alone. She had the support of the Reshian, others with shadow ability.

The Hjan fell back.

Some tried to flicker, but failed.

Carth's knife found home again and again. With each attack, the anger she felt at losing her parents, anger she'd known from the day the Hjan had destroyed her family, faded. All she knew was the need to continue her attack, the need to expel the Hjan from Nyaesh.

Shadows swirled around her, filling her with power.

Then everything stopped.

Silence surrounded her.

She turned, noting the Reshian still nearby. They looked at her, watching for a moment, and then, with a swirl of shadows, they disappeared from the grounds.

That left only Carth.

The Hjan were gone, either disappeared with a flicker or dead. The A'ras pushed on the barrier she held, and Carth's strength faded. With another push, the barrier fell. Landon raced toward her, followed by other A'ras. Even Alison was with him.

Carth fell back and nearly stumbled.

There was nothing she could do. Nothing she could say. To them, she was a traitor. She had sided with the Reshian when she'd destroyed the Hjan.

Carth reached for the shadows, trying to pull them around her, but she had spent too much effort defeating the Hjan. Reaching for the A'ras magic, trying to find the flame as it burned within her, didn't get her any further.

Landon approached, leading the rest of the ashai and a few bloody A'ras. He stepped closer to her, the rest of the ashai remaining behind him. Carth waited for Alison to step forward, or Samis, but neither did.

As Landon neared, nausea rolled through her.

"Landon?" she said.

He frowned at her, leaning close enough that she could smell his breath.

"The Hjan attacked us."

He shook his head. "Harrison signed an agreement with them. There was going to be peace. And now you've ruined it."

"This wasn't me! The Reshian helped us."

"You're not even of Nyaesh. You know nothing, Rel. And now you won't matter. Harrison should have done this when he learned of your treachery."

He slipped his sword forward.

Carth took in a deep breath, drawing the shadows with her, and rolled to the side. With one last effort, she kicked, driving the heel of her boot out at his hand, and heard a satisfying crack. Without thinking, she lunged, driving the serrated edge of the knife Invar had given her toward his stomach, pushing the shadows out as she did.

She froze.

If she did that, she would be every bit the traitor they believed.

Landon staggered back, his hand dropping to his stomach.

One of the ashai—Alison, she noted with horror—caught him.

Carth watched, wanting to go to her friend, wanting to return to the ashai, but what could she do? To them, she had proven herself Reshian now, and she had almost killed Landon. She imagined similar stories coming out about her killing the masters. Invar might know the truth, but would others believe him? They thought him addled, thought that his mind had begun to slip. Any help she could get there was doubtful.

Even the hope of her friends supporting her faded. Not only Alison, but now Samis and one of the remaining A'ras crouched around Landon, helping him back up. As she watched, they turned to her, even Alison and Samis looking at her with hatred in their eyes.

Carth scrambled back, drawing the shadow cloak around her. Each step brought her closer to the wall, and farther from the home she'd known for the last five years.

All she'd wanted was to fit in. To understand how to use the A'ras magic. To have a place where she belonged, a home.

Nyaesh would not be her home now. It could not be.

As she reached the wall, she disappeared.

Chapter 27

Carth was walking around the wall, tracing her hand along the stone, when she felt a soft burning of A'ras magic. She looked up, afraid of who she might find. She was in no place to defend herself, too weakened by the attack. After what had happened, she should leave the city, should leave the palace at least, but she couldn't bring herself to do it. As much as she recognized that she no longer belonged here, it was too hard to tear herself from this place.

"You did well, Ms. Rel."

Invar. He was thinner than before, his face pale as if he'd lost blood during the fight. A dark cloak hung around his shoulders and his face wore a serious expression.

"I have to leave, Invar."

He took a step toward her. His gait was off and he staggered a little. "Yes. You do."

"They think the Hjan fought the Reshian. They think the Reshian attacked the A'ras."

He breathed out slowly, and his arms fell to his sides. "The Hjan mimicked the Reshian shadows when they appeared. They furthered a war that had only simmered, Ms. Rel. Now most within the palace grounds believe the attack *was* Reshian. We know the difference, but…"

She didn't need him to explain that no one would believe either of them.

"The masters made it difficult for you to remain, Ms. Rel. When they offered a bargain to the Hjan, there could be no other outcome."

"I don't understand what happened."

Invar motioned for her to follow, and they started into the city. Carth noted that they traveled along Doland Road, which would take them to the docks. Fitting that she should go this way.

"The Reshian have known about the Hjan presence in Nyaesh for some time. The initial attacks were meant to draw the Hjan off the palace grounds, but they discovered something else."

"What?"

He looked over at her. "You, Ms. Rel. You revealed your shadow ability to them, and the Reshian knew that they needed to destroy the shadow barrier around the grounds."

"This was about me?"

"Not only you, but partly. I suspect they believed they needed to reclaim you. To do that, the Reshian wanted to destroy the protections around the palace. They have fought the A'ras for many years, but that story is for a different time. When they learned of the alliance with the Hjan, the Reshian had no choice but to attack."

Carth thought of how many had died. Not only the

Reshian, but also the A'ras. "We... I killed them."

They reached River Road. The noise of the city faded and the sounds of the docks nearly overwhelmed her.

"That was not you, Ms. Rel. You did what was necessary. You saved lives that night, much as you did when you fought today."

She swallowed. "I won't ever be A'ras, will I, Invar?"

He offered a sad smile. "Ms. Rel, you were never meant to be A'ras." He stopped near a massive ship with sails that was rolling in. Men worked along the deck, pulling lines and readying for arrival. "You needed to learn from the A'ras, but that was only a step in your journey."

It was similar to what Jhon had said to her.

With that thought, a man separated from the darkness between the buildings leading to the dock. He was slight of build and had a plain, youthful face. Jhon.

"I think you know him, Ms. Rel?"

"Jhon?"

He nodded. "It is time for the next step in your training, I think, Carthenne. Are you ready?"

Carth looked back toward the palace. Even if she wasn't ready, she couldn't return. That option was closed to her, much as returning to the Wounded Lyre had been closed to her before.

She sensed that she didn't have to go with Jhon, but what else would she do? She wanted to learn about her abilities, wanted to know what they meant for her. The only way to do that was by going with him.

"If I do this, where are we going?"

"There are other places for you to learn, other steps on your journey. In that way, you are like the wall surrounding the palace, both ivy and stone. You have learned one aspect of your abilities, and Jhon... he can help you learn the other."

"The Reshian?" she asked.

"There are some who would help you understand," Jhon said. "When we find them, you can learn what it means that you can use the shadows the way you do."

She looked toward the palace. Were the Hjan still out there? She'd pushed them back, so she didn't think so, but they were *somewhere*. With their ability to flicker, they could appear anywhere. If she could stay here, she could help protect the city... but that was no longer an option for her.

"We should attack them," she said softly. "We should see the Hjan destroyed."

Jhon glanced at Invar, and a strange, worried expression flitted across their faces before fading. "You should learn first," he said.

Carth closed her eyes. What choice did she have but to go with him? She *wanted* to learn to control her power, but leaving Nyaesh felt too much like running.

What could she do without knowing her powers? To become strong enough to stop the Hjan—to really stop them—she would have to become as Invar said, like the wall around the palace, both stone and ivy. She didn't know which represented the shadows and which the A'ras, but she had to know enough to use the combination to be stronger than either.

When Jhon stepped to the side, she hesitated only a moment more before letting him lead her onto the ship, and finally away from Nyaesh.

END

Acknowledgements:

I want to thank all the people who helped me get this book together, including all my awesome beta readers, West of Mars editing, Clio Editing, Polgarus Studios for print formatting, my fantastic cover designer, and mostly, my family for allowing me the time to do the work!

About the Author:

New York Times and USA Today Bestselling Author D.K. Holmberg lives in Minnesota and is the author of multiple series including The Cloud Warrior Saga, The Dark Ability, The Endless War, and The Lost Garden. When he's not writing, he's chasing around his two active children.

Check my website for updates and new releases:
http://www.dkholmberg.com.

Follow me on Facebook:
www.facebook.com/dkholmberg

I'm occasionally on twitter:
www.twitter.com/dkholmberg

Also By DK Holmberg

The Endless War
Journey of Fire and Night
Darkness Rising
Endless Night
Summoner's Bond
Seal of Light

The Dark Ability
The Dark Ability
The Heartstone Blade
The Tower of Venass
Blood of the Watcher
The Shadowsteel Forge
The Guild Secret
Rise of the Elder

The Shadow Accords
Shadow Blessed
Shadow Cursed
Shadow Born

The Sighted Assassin
The Painted Girl
The Binders Game

The Forgotten
Assassin's End

The Cloud Warrior Saga
Chased by Fire
Bound by Fire
Changed by Fire
Fortress of Fire
Forged in Fire
Serpent of Fire
Servant of Fire
Born of Fire
Broken of Fire
Light of Fire

The Lost Garden
Keeper of the Forest
The Desolate Bond
Keeper of Light

Made in the USA
San Bernardino, CA
15 March 2017